"I just don't think friends should do this to each other," muttered Angela.

"Gymnastics?" asked Linda, blinking her big blue eyes.

"No. Boy stealing," said Angela hotly.

"Boy stealing?" exclaimed Terri. "Bobby's not your personal property, Angela."

"Yeah. Until it's official that you're his girlfriend, you can't make us stop liking him or talking to him," said Linda.

Sonya sat with a dreamy expression on her face. "He's the kind of boy who loves you for who you are. Do you know what I mean?" she asked her friends.

Angela narrowed her eyes and shot angry stares at her friend. "Okay, Benedict Arnold. If Bobby likes you for who you are right now, he should have his head examined." She jumped up and ran out of the house, with her friends yelling at her to come back—please.

Books by Susan Smith

Samantha Slade #1: Samantha Slade: Monster Sitter
Samantha Slade #2: Confessions of a Teen-age Frog
Samantha Slade #3: Our Friend: Public Nuisance #1
Samantha Slade #4: The Terrors of Rock and Roll

Available from ARCHWAY Paperbacks

Best Friends #1: Sonya Begonia and the Eleventh Birthday Blues
Best Friends #2: Angela and the King-Size Crusade
Best Friends #3: Dawn Selby, Super Sleuth
Best Friends #4: Terri the Great
Best Friends #5: Sonya and the Chain Letter Gang
Best Friends #6: Angela and the Greatest Guy in the World

Available from MINSTREL Books

#6 Angela and the
Greatest Guy in the World

by
Susan Smith

A MINSTREL® BOOK

PUBLISHED BY POCKET BOOKS

New York   London   Toronto   Sydney   Tokyo

A MINSTREL PAPERBACK *ORIGINAL*

A Minstrel Book published by
POCKET BOOKS, a division of Simon & Schuster, Inc.
1230 Avenue of the Americas, New York, NY 10020

ISBN: 0-671-68161-3

First Minstrel Books printing December 1989

10 9 8 7 6 5 4 3 2 1

A MINSTREL BOOK and colophon are registered trademarks of
Simon & Schuster Inc.

Printed in the U.S.A.

For Annabelle

Chapter One

"Wow!" muttered Angela King under her breath. She stopped in her tracks in the lobby of the Gladstone Twinplex Movie Theater, scooped her dark curly hair out of her eyes, and stared straight ahead at a gorgeous-looking boy.

Her four best friends, Terri, Sonya, Dawn, and Linda, plowed into her, nearly knocking her down, but she hardly noticed.

"Angie, what're you doing?" blurted out Terri Rivera, the loudest mouth of the group.

Dawn Selby, the smallest of the girls, held her chest with concern. "I feel flattened," she cried.

"That should save money on B-R-A-S," said Terri, giggling.

Dawn turned bright red. "Shhh!"

Angela stared at the tall, lanky boy with green eyes and tousled curly blond hair. He walked, or rather, loped, toward the exit with assurance, as though he were headed somewhere very important.

"Wow," she mumbled again, starting toward the exit.

"What's with you?" demanded Sonya Plummer. She pushed her brown bangs out of her eyes to get a better look at her friend. "You look like you're hypnotized. Terri, you're the expert on hypnotism. What's wrong with Angela?"

Terri rolled her eyes in exasperation. "Pul-lease! I can't stand hypnotism—it's a farce!" Terri's mother was working on a documentary film about the sixth sense. Terri was completely turned off and didn't believe in hypnotism, psychics, or anything like that. She waved her palm in front of Angela's eyes, but Angela just blinked.

"Did you see that guy?" she asked her friends absently.

"What guy?" they chorused, scanning the lobby.

But the gorgeous guy had disappeared from view.

"The only guy in here is Mr. Tibbs behind the candy counter," said Sonya. "I'm sure you don't mean him."

"Yeah. Mr. Tibbs is married and has three kids," said Dawn. "I'm sure his wife wouldn't be too happy about all this."

"He's gone," Angela said, turning to look at them with disappointment.

"Who?"

"The greatest guy in the world," she replied, letting out a long sigh. He was so cute. How could they have missed him?

Terri sputtered.

"How can you say that?" Dawn asked. "You don't even like boys yet!" Dawn didn't like boys yet, either.

"Let me get this straight," said Terri, pacing up and down in front of her friend. Her dark hair, cut so short it stuck up in spikes, didn't even move as she ran back and forth. "You saw a boy here that you don't even know, and now he's the greatest guy in the world?"

"Yes!" Angela beamed. All four of her friends were looking at her as if birds were flying out of her ears. "What's wrong with that?"

"Now I've heard everything," said Linda Carmichael, shaking her pretty blond head in amazement. Linda was the girls' newest friend, and was known for not being easily surprised. "You sure are full of surprises, Angela."

Angela walked outside the theater ahead of the others, hoping to catch a glimpse of the boy. The theater was located in the Gladstone Mall, and lots of people were milling about, but there was no sign of the greatest guy. "I probably won't ever see him again," she said mournfully.

"Maybe not, but you will find another one just like him sometime," said Sonya, pulling Angela along by the elbow. "Come on, let's get an ice-cream sundae."

The girls hopped up on the pink- and white-striped stools in their new favorite ice-cream shop, Sundaze. Although Angela had dieted and lost all the weight she needed to, she still watched what she ate. She ordered a frozen yogurt, while her friends ordered sundaes piled high with whipped cream and nuts.

She pulled a piece of paper from her sweatshirt pocket. "I cut this out of the newspaper," she told the others. "It's an advertisement for an acting class."

The girls passed the article around. Angela kept talking. "Since we want to do something for the Spring Fling Talent Show, this class could help us be the very best!"

"Great idea!" cried Sonya, who was in charge of the committee to organize the show. "I think we should all join."

"Yeah, me, too," said Terri. "What're we doing for the show, by the way?"

"Some kind of a skit," suggested Angela. "That way we can all do it together and work as a team."

"Sounds like fun," said Linda, wiping a drip of ice cream from her chin. "I've never acted before."

"You've acted silly," said Sonya, tickling Linda in the ribs so hard that she nearly fell off her stool.

Angela, Terri, and Dawn started laughing.

"We don't need a class to learn how to act silly," spluttered Dawn.

"Okay, okay, stop!" cried Linda, tears rolling down her cheeks. "What's this skit going to be about?"

"Who knows? We'll make up the whole thing," suggested Angela.

"But first let's make sure we don't let Celia Forester know we're taking the class," warned Sonya. "Or else, she'll want to take it, too, and we don't want her in there."

"That's right. We want our skit to be the very best in the whole show," agreed Terri.

"I think we should ask our parents tonight if we can take the class," said Angela. "It's not very expensive, so we all have a chance."

"And besides, we can tell them it'll teach us how to act right," Sonya added, giggling. With that, she moved her elbow, nudging her entire sundae into her lap.

"Fat chance," said Terri, shaking her head while the others shrieked with laughter.

After getting their parents' permission, Angela and her friends made plans to go to their first acting class on Monday after school.

When the last bell of the day rang, Angela was so excited, she could hardly stop herself from running down the hall to meet the others. She loved acting, and she had an important role in the school production of *West Side Story*. But Celia had played the lead, and that was the reason Angela didn't want Celia to find out about this acting class. Celia was already a good actress, the prettiest girl in the sixth grade, and also the most conceited, as far as Angela was concerned. She didn't need acting lessons to help her.

Angela and her friends rode their bikes to the class. The class was located about fifteen minutes from Gladstone Elementary by bicycle. Everything in Gladstone, a small California town, was within easy distance of everything else—even the mountains and the beach.

Angela was the first to dart into the building. Terri, who was usually first anywhere, was only a close second this time.

As soon as Angela pushed through the inner door, she stopped and gasped out loud. Across the room was the boy from the Gladstone Triplex—the greatest guy in the world! He was standing right across from her, grinning at her, his green eyes almost hidden under locks of curly blond hair. She grinned back.

Just then, Sonya came up behind her and obviously saw him, too. She didn't gasp—she dropped her backpack on Angela's shoe, instead.

"Ouch!" Angela said, rubbing her foot.

"Sorry, Angie," Sonya replied, not taking her eyes from the boy.

"She probably has a week's supply of clothes in that bag," said Terri.

"Terri!" hissed Sonya, her face flushing with embarrassment. Sonya was crazy about clothes and did usually carry a change in her pack.

"Hi, class." The teacher, Ms. Bergman, interrupted them just then. She was an elegant, middle-aged lady with black and gray hair that she wore short. Right away Angela liked the way she made great, sweeping gestures with her hands.

After introducing herself, she said, "And now I'd like each of you to tell us your name and what school you come from. Let's start with you, Bobby."

Bobby. So that was his name, thought Angela.

"I'm Bobby Bugrin, and right now I go to the Robert Louis School, but I might transfer," he explained, looking straight at Angela.

She thought she would melt. She was so busy staring at Bobby that Linda had to nudge her when it was her turn to speak.

"Angela, wake up," she hissed.

"Oh, uh, Angela K-King, from Gladstone Elementary School," she stammered, feeling her face grow hot and red.

Bobby's grin grew wider as the rest of the class introduced themselves.

"Now, what we're going to do first is read a bit from Rudyard Kipling's *Just So Stories,* just to see how well you read," said Ms. Bergman, smiling at each student in turn.

"Okay, each of you will read a paragraph from the story, 'The Elephant's Child,' please."

She handed the story to Terri, and she read in a loud clear voice, " 'In the High and Far-off Times the Elephant, O Best Beloved, had no trunk. He had only a blackish, bulgy nose, as big as a boot, that he could wriggle from side to side, but he couldn't pick up things with it. . . .' "

Angela was next. Bobby was still staring at her, and she could barely concentrate. " 'But there was one Elephant—a new Elephant—an Elephant's Child—who was full of 'satiable curiosity, and that means he asked ever so many questions. . . .' "

Sonya nudged Angela when she was done. "Too bad Howard isn't here," she whispered. "He could do the sound effects." Howard Tarter, Sonya's sort-of-boyfriend, had visited Africa with his parents and had memorized all jungle-animal sounds.

After everyone had read a part of the story, Ms. Bergman said she wanted each of them to mimic an animal from the jungle. The boys instantly started to clown around, pretending to be monkeys. Ms. Bergman stopped them by telling each person what she wanted him or her to be. Angela was to be a rhinoceros, Terri a crocodile, Sonya a giraffe, Dawn an ostrich, and Linda an elephant.

"Am I an elephant before or after I get my trunk?" Linda asked, and everyone laughed.

"You choose," said Ms. Bergman, joining in the laughter.

Linda made great elephant noises and decided to use her arm as her trunk.

Terri wriggled along the floor like a crocodile, snapping her jaws as though she were planning to eat someone. As a giraffe, Sonya stretched her neck out. Dawn ran around the room fast, as ostriches do, and then stuck her head in a corner because there wasn't a handy hole in the floor.

Then it was Angela's turn. As a rhinoceros, she decided to charge, so she stuck out her finger from the top of her head and charged toward the group of kids on the other side of the room. Everyone scooted out of her way, shrieking and laughing. Everyone, that is, except Bobby, who zigged when he should have zagged. Angela ran smack into his stomach with a dull thud.

"Uh," she groaned, her head starting to pound.

The class laughed.

"What a way to go, Angela!" cried Terri, clapping.

Angela stood up slowly, holding her head as Bobby held his stomach. "Hey, you've got a hard head," he said, grinning.

She grinned back, feeling embarrassed, sore, and happy all at the same time. That was the most romantic thing anyone had ever said to her. But all she could think to say to him was "Hi, I'm Angela."

"I don't know whether to say it's nice to meet you, or not," said Bobby, laughing.

She shrugged, but she couldn't stop smiling and blushing. He was even cuter when he talked than when he just stood there. This was the very first time she had ever felt this way about a boy, and it felt like the very first time she dove off the high-board.

When Angela turned around, she saw that all the girls were staring at Bobby. The boys were laughing about one of them jumping like a frog and had lost interest in Bobby and her.

When the class was over and everyone was filing out of the room, Sonya turned to Angela.

"Who was that guy you ran into in class?" she asked. "He was cute."

"Yeah, Angie," said Linda. "He's a hunk."

Angela looked at them in surprise. "You know his name— it's Bobby Bugrin. And he's mine," she added possessively. "I saw him first."

Terri, Linda, Sonya, and Dawn started laughing.

"I wonder if he knows he's yours," Terri said, running ahead.

"Yeah, I wonder, too. Bobby, did you know you belong to Angela?" whispered Dawn, giggling.

Linda was straining her neck to get a glimpse of Bobby as he climbed into his father's car.

Angela frowned and stuck her hands on her hips. "He's the greatest guy in the world, the one I saw at the theater the other day,'' she explained. Then she added, ''Before *any* of you saw him.''

Linda, Sonya, and Dawn jumped onto their bikes and followed Terri out of the parking lot. Angela couldn't forget Bobby. Even if she could stop thinking about him, she had a sore spot on her head to make her remember.

Chapter Two

⚏

"That acting job was so much fun," Angela said the next day, Tuesday, on the way to school.

Angela, Terri, and Dawn usually rode their bikes to school, which took them about fifteen minutes. Terri made the trip in ten minutes because she rode really fast and never stopped to talk as the others did. Sometimes, Linda would join them—if she could get going in time.

"Maybe we should be animals for our skit," suggested Dawn. "But I won't be an ostrich, though."

"Yeah. Speaking with your head buried in the sand would be hard," said Angela.

When they got to school, the first person they saw was Celia Forester. She was flouncing up and down the hallway, her long red-gold hair tied back with a blue ribbon. She was wearing a new blue sweat suit that the ribbon matched exactly.

"Oooh, Celia, you look so cute!" cried Polly Clinker, one of Celia's best friends.

"I like you in blue," said Jeannie Sandlin, Celia's other best friend.

"I think I'm going to be sick," said Terri, pretending to stick a finger down her throat before darting into homeroom.

Ms. Bell, the homeroom teacher, read the morning announcements and finished with, "Those students who wish to sign up for the Spring Fling Talent Show please see Sonya Plummer or Ms. Kerry."

Celia glared at Sonya, then raised her hand. "I can't tell anyone what I'm doing for the talent show, Ms. Bell," she said.

"Please discuss that with Ms. Kerry or Sonya, not me, Celia," said Ms. Bell.

Sonya raised her hand. "You can't have a secret talent for the show because we have to know how to organize all the acts."

"That's right," added Howard Tarter, the class president. Howard was short and dark-haired with glasses. He was also the funniest boy in the sixth grade.

"And how can Sonya organize the show if *some* people won't cooperate?" said Angela, giving Celia a hard look.

Ms. Bell, whom Angela thought of as the perfectionist teacher, sighed and patted her perfect curls. "All right, class. I suggest you have a meeting sometime after school to discuss this matter."

After class Celia sidled up to Angela and Sonya. "You know, if I want to have a secret act in the talent show, I'll have one."

"Is it going to be such a big secret that nobody even sees it?" Angela asked.

"No, but nobody's going to know what it is until it premieres," said Celia snootily.

"Sounds like trouble, if you ask me," said Terri as the girls walked to their new class.

When Angela got home that afternoon, she found her mother flipping through her closet, looking for something to wear to a local press buffet that night.

"Oh, Angela, I'm glad you're here. You can help me. Since I lost weight, I don't have anything to wear that doesn't look like a gunnysack," Mrs. King twittered, haphazardly sliding hangers back and forth on the long rod.

Mrs. King used to be heavy, until Angela went on a diet. Then her mother, a food critic and writer for *Food Sense* magazine, began to lose weight in spite of her job, which required her to sample all different sorts of foods.

"Mom, wear this," Angela said, grabbing a royal blue dress with a matching wide belt. "This looks good on you."

"You're right. Thanks, honey." Mrs. King slipped the dress over her head and adjusted it until it looked right. "What're you wearing?"

"I don't know," Angela replied. She disappeared into her room and picked through her clothes, finally settling on a tomato-red sweater dress.

"That color is fantastic on you, Angie," said Mrs. King as she breezed into Angela's room. "You're going to knock 'em dead."

"Mom, this is just a boring old buffet, isn't it? Just a bunch of press people?" Angela sighed, fastening her hair with a silver barrette.

"Yes, it's probably all the same crowd," said Mrs. King. "But we'll have fun."

Angela and her mother had a really good relationship, and Angela felt especially proud of her mom because she had lost so much weight in spite of her job. But what Angela liked most about her mom was that she could easily talk to her about almost anything. A lot of girls her age couldn't talk to their moms.

Mrs. King and Angela talked about food all the way to the nearby hotel, where the buffet was held. Inside the banquet room, Angela recognized a lot of the faces in the party room from her years of having to attend these events with her mom. But all of a sudden, next to a potted palm plant, she saw a face she never expected to see—Bobby's face.

She gasped. "Bobby!"

"Angela!" he cried, looking totally surprised. "What're you doing here?"

A man rested a hand on Bobby's shoulder, smiling at Angela and Mrs. King. "I'll bet you're the daughter of the famous food critic, Ellen King. Am I right?"

"Uh, yes," said Angela, blushing.

"This is the girl who knocked me over in acting class, Dad," said Bobby. "She was being a rhinoceros."

"What a pretty rhinoceros," remarked Mr. Bugrin, smiling at Angela.

Angela was sensitive to being called anything big, since she had once been called "Fatso" around school. But she decided Mr. Bugrin didn't mean anything bad by it.

Mrs. King laughed. "And this, Angela, is Ross Bugrin. He's with the Gladstone *Times.*"

They all shook hands, and then Mrs. King helped herself to a canape.

"Oh, you must try these, Ross," she exclaimed. "They're wonderful—they just melt on your tongue."

"What a recommendation!" Mr. Bugrin said, chuckling. He tasted one of the canapes.

"Oh, and one of these little sausage rolls, I really shouldn't have any, but I must try just one," Mrs. King went on, daintily popping the smallest of the sausage rolls into her mouth. "The pastry is so airy. It's really fine."

"The way you talk about food makes me want to fill my plate," said Mr. Bugrin.

Angela saw him give her mom a quick wink and knew he really liked her. She was glad.

Bobby cleared his throat. "Well, do you want to stand around here, or do you want to get a soda?"

"A soda, definitely." As they walked to the drink table, she talked to cover an awkward silence. "Usually, there's nobody my age at these things."

"Yeah, that's what I usually find. I'm surprised I didn't see you around before our class," Bobby said, smiling at her. She noticed he had a soft, drawly way of talking.

Angela felt that excited, high-dive feeling again, right in the pit of her stomach, and couldn't speak.

Bobby picked up two sodas and handed her one. "Well," he said, and then, "Well," again. "What do you like to do besides charge into people?"

She giggled and blushed. "I like acting, singing, bike riding, horseback riding. Lots of stuff."

"Yeah, me, too. I like those things, too—bike riding, singing, acting," he said, grinning. "I've been in a couple of school plays."

"So have I," she said. Then she told him about the Spring Fling Talent Show. "That's why my friends and I joined the acting class."

"I just hope we don't have to pretend to be animals forever in class," said Bobby. "I was hoping to play a human being sometime."

"Yeah, me, too." Angela stared at the toes of her red flats, not knowing what to say next.

"Do you want to get some food?" he asked.

Angela didn't want to get anything because she was afraid

she'd eat five of every item. But she said okay, and wandered back to the buffet table.

Mr. Bugrin and Mrs. King were still standing together and smiled as their children approached. Mr. Bugrin was tall and blond, and Angela could see where Bobby got his good looks.

"Oh, Angie, do try the wontons, they're delectable," Mrs. King insisted.

"Mom, they'll make me weigh one ton," moaned Angela. Bobby laughed. "Hey, that's funny."

"There are vegetables, too. They've arranged everything like a garden of flowers on that platter," said Mrs. King, pointing to a beautiful tray of raw vegetables.

"Ellen, you do have a way with words," said Mr. Bugrin. "You've persuaded me to eat enough to feed an army."

"Nonsense, Ross," said Mrs. King, patting his shoulder. "You're as slim as a string bean. You could eat enough for three armies and it wouldn't affect you."

"I've been meaning to tell you, Ellen, how lovely you look," Mr. Bugrin said, and Angela noticed that her mother turned suddenly red.

Her mom was blushing? she thought. Well, Mr. Bugrin was being awfully nice to her, and she didn't seem to mind.

When Mrs. King finally announced that it was time to leave, Bobby smiled at Angela. "Well, I guess I'll see you in acting class."

"Yeah. I won't knock you over next time," she said.

"Is that a promise?" he asked seriously, and then followed it with a quick wink.

Angela and Mrs. King said goodbye and made their way toward the exit. Angela felt warm all over as she slid into the car beside her mother.

"Had a good time, honey?" Mrs. King asked her, patting her hand a little distractedly.

"Yeah, it was fun," replied Angela.

"I've known Ross for years," Mrs. King went on. "I knew him before his divorce, and he seems changed somehow. And Bobby seems like such a nice boy. . . ."

Angela half listened, for she was thinking about Bobby. She kept replaying her conversation with him over and over until she had every expression and every word memorized.

She couldn't wait to tell her friends.

Chapter Three

⌘

Angela was late getting to school the next day and then she had a dental appointment during lunch, so she wouldn't have a chance to talk to her friends until after school. But first she had a meeting to get through. She thought she was going to pop with the news about Bobby.

"I call this meeting to order!" shouted Howard, pounding on the desk with a banana because he didn't have a gavel.

Everyone giggled, but stopped talking.

"We have to talk about the Spring Fling Talent Show," Howard announced. "Now, Sonya, you tell us what's going on."

Sonya stood up in front of the others. That day's meeting consisted of Sonya, Howard, Angela, Terri, Dawn, Tommy Atwood, Polly, and Jeannie. Celia had ballet practice so she had to miss the meeting.

"Everyone who wants to be in the show has to tell us what they'll be doing during the next week," Sonya explained. "And that means everyone, so tell Celia about it, so we can start planning.'' She looked pointedly at Jeannie and Polly, who nodded their heads up and down.

''Next we need people to work on sets and props,'' she went on.

All hands shot up in the air, except Polly's. ''I don't like making things,'' she explained. ''I don't like the smell of glue.''

Terri made a loud noise through her nose. ''Well, you're not supposed to sniff it, Polly.''

''I don't do that, Terri,'' Polly said with disgust.

Everyone laughed.

''Okay, as soon as we know what everybody is going to do, we can talk about designing the sets,'' said Sonya.

''I can design the sets,'' offered Tommy, the boy Terri liked.

''I didn't know you liked to design sets,'' Terri exclaimed. Tommy turned beet-red.

Terri and Tommy were both sports crazy, but obviously Terri didn't know about Tommy's interest in art and design.

After the meeting Angela rode home with Terri, Dawn, and Sonya, who was going to Terri's house. Once they were five minutes from the school, she told them about Bobby being at the buffet.

Sonya's bike screeched to a halt, her brown hair flying into her face. ''Really? How could you keep this from us?'' she demanded.

''There wasn't a good time to tell you before now,'' said Angela. ''And the best part is my mother knows his father,'' she added.

''Oh, that's sweet,'' said Terri. ''Will you go on double dates?''

Angela wrinkled her nose in disgust. ''With our *parents?*''

Dawn giggled. "That would be funny. Anyway, you're too young to date, Angie."

"Howard and I went on a movie date," offered Sonya.

"It wasn't really a date," Angela said. "You met each other there."

"Yes, but we planned it. That means it's a date," Sonya insisted.

Terri rolled her eyes. "Will you guys cut it out? Just go home and look up *date* in the dictionary. That's the best way to settle this," she said, pedaling ahead of them.

On Thursday the girls went to their second acting class. This time Angela wore an orangish sweater and dark green pants, one of her favorite outfits.

"You look like an orange tree," Terri observed as they were turning their bikes into the parking lot beside their class.

"Thanks," said Angela, sticking her arms out like branches. She had to grab the handlebars in a hurry to avoid being bounced off by a pothole.

They all parked and ran in together to find Bobby already there. Terri left the group standing just inside the door and marched straight up to him.

"If we do scenes today, d'you want to do one with me?" she asked, grinning up at him.

Angela's mouth fell open in shock. Were her eyes playing tricks? Was Terri *flirting?*

Bobby turned bright red, but he nodded. "If we do scenes and if the teacher says it's okay." Then he looked up and over Terri's head to smile straight at Angela.

Angela was so angry at Terri, she couldn't even smile back. Her face wouldn't budge from its mad expression. Bobby turned away from Terri and started talking to some boys. How could Terri do that? She was supposed to like *Tommy!*

Ms. Bergman lined them all up and arranged them in pairs, making sure one person out of each pair could sing well. Dawn and Angela were together.

"You're going to do a scene from *Phantom of the Opera,*" explained Ms. Bergman. She put on the record so they could become familiar with the piece of music.

Angela noticed that Terri had been paired with Bobby. Well, he could sing and Terri couldn't, so that made sense, Angela decided. Terri did the talking part. Angela listened while Bobby sang the song. He had a very good voice.

Then it was her turn. She closed her eyes and imagined herself in the part and sang as well as she could, letting the melody pour out of her. She loved the music. It made her skin prickle with goose bumps.

"Wonderful, Angela," Ms. Bergman praised her.

Out of the corner of her eye, Angela could see Bobby looking at her. Did he like her singing? She hoped so.

After everyone had performed, Ms. Bergman chose Bobby to play the phantom. He was to hide behind the closet doors and burst out, scaring everyone, when they least expected him to.

"Ahhhh!" shrieked Dawn, jumping a foot off the floor when he leaped out at them.

Angela, Linda, Terri, and Sonya gasped and took off in separate directions. Dawn stood shaking, until Angela came back and grabbed her by the hand to whisk her off to her corner of the room.

"Very good, class!" exclaimed Ms. Bergman, clapping her hands together. "We'll meet again next week, and in the meantime, I want you to study this script." She handed a black notebook to each person.

"We have to study this *and* think of something for our talent show," moaned Sonya, pushing through the doors to the outside. "I'll be an overworked actress before I'm twelve."

"And an underpaid one," said Terri, gazing after Bobby as he strolled toward his father's car.

Angela noticed Terri and pulled her away from the others. "Okay, why did you ask Bobby to do a scene with you?" she demanded.

"Because I wanted to," returned Terri.

"But aren't you supposed to be madly in love with Tommy?" Angela asked.

"Tommy and I have a purely professional relationship," insisted Terri. "And this is the same thing. I'm not interested in romance."

"Oh, yeah, sure," scoffed Angela. "We've all heard *that* one before."

"It's true!" cried Terri hotly.

"Anyway, you and I are friends, and that's supposed to come first. I told you *I* liked Bobby, so I thought you would leave him alone," said Angela.

"Well, I can be friends with him," Terri said. "There's nothing wrong with that."

"Friends! You don't pay any attention to guys unless you really like them," Linda pointed out, joining Terri and Angela with Sonya and Dawn.

"Yeah," agreed Angela. "Tommy and Bobby are the only boys you've ever looked at."

"How do you know?" Terri cried. "Do you follow me around and take notes?"

"You know what I mean. You were flirting with Bobby and you won't admit it," Angela said, her voice rising.

"You don't *own* Bobby, Angela," Terri said, sticking her face right up close to Angela's.

"Maybe not, but I wouldn't do this to you," Angela replied, pinching her nose shut with her fingertips so she didn't have to smell Terri's bubble gum breath.

"Angie, he's just a boy," Dawn reminded her gently.

"Right. He's not worth it," said Linda.

"Yeah. When are you going to learn that boys are no big deal?" asked Terri, throwing her hands up in the air. Then she jumped on her bike and rode away.

"It would still be nice if you said you were sorry!" Angela yelled after her.

Terri turned around in her seat. "What for? I didn't do anything wrong!"

Angela watched her, still fuming. Maybe all her friends were right. Maybe she was making a big deal over nothing. She hated arguing like this. But as she climbed onto her bike, she was still mad and still thought Terri was wrong.

Chapter Four

⚘

"Only Ms. Kerry knows what my group is doing," sneered Celia. "And you won't be learning anything, either, because we're not even going to rehearse here."

Angela, Dawn, Howard, Celia, and Sonya were standing on the stage in the auditorium, talking about the talent show.

"Celia, how are we going to make sets for you if we don't know what you're doing?" demanded Sonya.

"Don't worry about it," Celia replied in the same snotty tone.

"You have to let us know pretty soon, Celia, or else you'll have to do your act in the aisle," said Howard.

"The only thing I'll say about it is Gilbert and Sullivan," said Celia, grinning widely.

"That leaves us about twenty Gilbert and Sullivan operettas to choose from," groaned Angela, who knew something about plays. "Not to mention the number of scenes."

"About a thousand scenes," added Howard, who knew something about everything.

"Well, have fun figuring it all out," Celia said gaily. She

flipped her shiny red hair over her shoulder and strolled out of the auditorium.

Angela shook her head. "Her parents are probably buying her professional sets. Yikes! Who grabbed me?"

Dawn and Sonya hid themselves in the stage curtain and were trying to poke everyone who stood near them.

"Ow, what's that?" cried Howard, raising his arms in front of his face and pretending to be terrified.

"Look behind you," Angela told him, giggling.

Howard ran around in a circle, screaming like a maniac. "It's the curtain monsters. Aaaaah!"

Laughter exploded from the moving curtains, then Angela and Howard sneaked up on the curtain monsters and tried to tickle them to death.

When Angela got home, she noticed Mr. Bugrin's business card on the table next to the phone. The telephone number on it was one for the *Times*. Angela had an idea. She leafed through the phone book and found the Bugrins' home phone number and address. But there was a problem—there were two Bugrins listed, Lisa and Ross. Did Bobby live with his mom or his dad? she wondered. In the short time she had known him, the subject had never come up.

She decided to ask her mother.

"I think Bobby lives with his father most of the time because his mother travels a lot," replied Mrs. King. "They have joint custody."

"Oh." Angela wrote down Ross Bugrin's home address. "Hey, Mom, I'm going for a bike ride."

"Okay, honey. Dinner will be a little late tonight, anyway," Mrs. King said.

Angela went out to the garage and climbed onto her ten-speed. She coasted down the hill, enjoying the sound of the gears clicking and the feel of the soft breeze in her hair as it was blown straight back. The countryside sped past her as she headed toward the beach, to the coast highway where Bobby lived. It took her almost an hour to get there.

Bobby's driveway was marked by a red, white, and blue mailbox with the name Bugrin written in the same colors. It looked almost as if a little kid had crayoned the name on the mailbox.

Angela didn't go down the driveway, but stopped at the head of it and just looked at the house.

The house, made of white stucco with red roof tiles, was perched on a cliff. Trees leaned against it as though they were afraid of falling over the cliff into the ocean. Angela guessed that the strong sea winds had blown them that way. On the front lawn, there were a skateboard and two tricycles. Bobby must have brothers or sisters, she guessed.

She started back the way she had come and had gone only a couple of blocks when she noticed a familiar-looking red bike in a rack outside a small park. It looked like Sonya's bike, even down to the crooked blue racing stripes Sonya had pasted on herself. Angela swung off her bike and strolled through the park. She spotted Sonya standing on a footbridge, which crossed a stream, feeding some ducks with popcorn she must have brought as a snack.

Angela shouted Sonya's name. Startled, Sonya dropped her bag of popcorn into the water, and the ducks attacked it. The thrashing and quacking made every park visitor turn to look at them and the girls.

"What're you doing here?" Sonya asked.

"I was just going to ask you the same question," Angela said, giving her a sidelong look.

"I went for a long bike ride and just happened to end up here," said Sonya, biting her lip.

Angela knew that when Sonya bit her lip like that, she wasn't telling the whole truth. "And you had no idea that Bobby lives a couple of blocks from here, right?"

"Well . . ." Sonya faltered.

"Well, what?" demanded Angela in a loud voice. "Is this where you always come for a bike ride?"

"Angie, stop yelling," said Sonya, frowning. "Even the ducks are looking at you."

"I thought *Howard* was your true love?" Angela persisted.

Sonya shrugged. "Well, he is. But I like Bobby, too."

"You're two-faced, Sonya," Angela yelled, feeling her face grow hot. "You can't like two boys at the same time! Especially when your best friend has claimed one of them!"

"Hey!" someone called.

Angela and Sonya turned at the sound of the boy's voice to see Bobby on his bike, waving at them from a short distance. He rode toward them.

"Hi, Bobby," Sonya said, smiling as though nothing had happened.

Angela frowned. She knew her face was bright red. "Hi, Bobby," she said.

"Hey, did I come by at a bad time or something?" he asked, glancing from Angela to Sonya.

"Uh, no," said Angela, looking down at her shoes. "Now is as good a time as any."

"I live just over there." He pointed in the direction of his house. "I come here to use the archery range."

Angela noticed the bow and quiver of arrows over his shoulder.

"Robin Hood, huh?" she asked.

"Yes. Except I don't steal from the rich to give to the poor," he told her, grinning.

"Have you ever played Robin Hood in a play?" asked

Sonya, smiling at him. She seemed to light up in front of Bobby.

"Nope," Bobby replied. "Did you ever shoot an arrow?"

Angela and Sonya wagged their heads and said no.

"Try it sometime," he suggested. "Well, I have to go meet somebody at the archery range. See you later."

"See you," Angela said.

"Bye," said Sonya, waving her fingers at him.

"I think I'm going to die of embarrassment," declared Angela as Bobby rode off down the bike path.

"Me, too," Sonya said. "He didn't hear what we were arguing about, did he?"

"Not unless he has scoops for ears. He was too far away," replied Angela. "But he knew we were fighting about something."

A park ranger approached them. "Did you girls drop that plastic bag in the water?" he asked.

"I did, by accident," Sonya admitted. "She surprised me."

Angela glared at her. "Oh, it's all my fault, huh?"

Sonya gave her a dirty look.

"Well, would you kindly go and get it? Plastic bags aren't good for the environment," said the ranger. "The ducks can choke on them."

"Sure, I'm sorry," said Sonya. She ran off the footbridge and grabbed a long branch to fish the bag out of the water. Holes had been bitten in the bag by the ducks, and all the popcorn was gone.

Angela came up beside her. "I wonder what Howard would think of this." Howard was planning to be an environmentalist when he grew up.

"Howard would think I was a wonderful person for making sure the ducks don't choke on the bag," Sonya replied.

Angela grabbed the bag and pointed at the holes. "But there are *bites* taken out of the bag, Sonya!"

Sonya placed her hands on her hips, exasperated. "Do you see any choking ducks, Angela?"

Angela gazed at the stream. All the ducks were swimming peacefully. Suddenly she thought about Sonya liking Bobby again. Her stomach felt queasy and a hard lump formed in her throat.

"I'm going home," she announced, walking away from her friend without looking at her.

"See you," called Sonya.

As Angela ran to her bike she remembered how Sonya had lost interest in Howard because she thought he wasn't romantic enough. And then she remembered the time that Sonya had become friends with Celia, even though Angela, Dawn, and Terri had warned her about Celia. The truth was, although Sonya was Angela's first and closest friend, she could be very unpredictable.

Hot tears gathered in Angela's eyes as she thought of how far apart she and Sonya were right then. Even though Sonya had seen her cry millions of times, she was glad that she couldn't see her now.

Chapter Five

❀

"Angela, you're sitting on the potato chips," said Terri.

"Oh, sorry," Angela replied, sitting up to pull the squashed chips out. How had she sat on it without hearing a crunch? she wondered.

It was Sunday afternoon. Angela, Terri, Linda, Sonya, and Dawn were sitting in front of the big-screen TV in Terri's living room, getting ready to watch a gymnastics performance that featured Linda, Terri, and unfortunately, Celia.

Dawn passed a bowl of M&M's around. Angela figured this was an ultra-special occasion, so she allowed herself one handful.

Terri fixed the reception on the TV while they waited for the program to begin. Sonya arranged her M&M's on a napkin in the pattern of a smiling face.

Linda leaped to her feet immediately. "Oh, I've got to call Bobby and tell him about the show. He'll want to see us, Terri."

"*Bobby?*" Angela and Sonya chorused, then glared at Linda.

"Sure. He's interested in our careers," explained Linda, moving toward the phone.

"But he doesn't even *know* you," protested Angela. "How can he care about your stupid careers?"

"Oh, so now Linda's and my careers are stupid?" Terri's eyes burned with indignation.

"I didn't mean that," Angela replied. "I just meant why should he care? He doesn't know you at all."

Angela noticed that Linda didn't have to look up Bobby's number. She had it memorized. All the girls fell silent to listen to Linda's end of the conversation.

"Oh, Bobby, hi. Listen. Terri and I are in a gymnastics competition on TV on Channel Nine in exactly five minutes. . . . Yeah. I think you'll like it. . . . Okay, 'bye." Linda put the receiver down and plopped down after she rejoined the others.

"There. He said he's going to turn the TV on right now. I knew he'd be interested." Linda tossed her long blond hair over her shoulder and crossed her legs in front of her.

"Oh, now you and Bobby are old friends?" demanded Angela.

"We can talk to Bobby, too, Angela," Terri told her.

"He's our friend, too," added Linda.

"Well, I think it stinks that you like the same boy I like," Angela said. "And now there are three of you. It's not fair." She glared at her friends.

"Angie, be quiet. The show's starting," said Dawn.

Angela hunched her body over her knees, her chin on her arms, and stared at the screen. Linda, Terri, and Celia cartwheeled into the center of the gym, wearing identical blue- and red-striped leotards. They looked very professional. Then to a popular song, each one did a separate routine.

Angela was furious. Of course Linda and Terri wanted

Bobby to see their show, to see what great gymnasts they were and how graceful they were. How could he not like them after seeing this? she wondered.

When it was over, they all clapped.

"Great, you guys," yelled Sonya. "You should be on TV more often."

"Or in the Olympics," suggested Dawn. "Then you'll get to go to some foreign country."

"With our luck, it would be held in Gladstone," said Terri, grinning.

"I just don't think friends should do this to one another," muttered Angela.

"Gymnastics?" asked Linda, blinking her big blue eyes.

"No. Boy stealing," said Angela hotly.

"Boy stealing?" exclaimed Terri. "Bobby's not your personal property, Angela."

"Yeah. Until it's official that you're his girlfriend, you can't make us stop liking him, or talking to him," said Linda.

Sonya sat with a dreamy expression on her face. "He's the kind of boy who likes you for who you are. Do you know what I mean?" she asked her friends.

Angela narrowed her eyes and shot angry stares at her friend. "Okay, Benedict Arnold. If Bobby likes you for who you are right now, he should have his head examined." She jumped up and ran out of the house, with her friends yelling at her to come back—please.

On Monday Angela decided to wear her best red and white sweat shirt to acting class. The five friends left right after school and rode directly to class.

"I got an idea for our skit," said Sonya as they pedaled easily along the street, five in a row.

"What?" asked Dawn.

"I call it—the monster skit. Three of us wear ugly masks and call ourselves the beautiful people. And the others wear no masks, and they're considered ugly."

"I like that idea," said Angela. Even though she was still mad at Sonya, she recognized a good idea when she heard one.

"Yeah, me, too," agreed Linda. "Then what happens?"

"The people in masks want to do plastic surgery on all the regular people," said Sonya.

"It makes you think about what beautiful is," said Angela.

"It's great," said Terri. "Do we have any lines?"

"Yes, I'll write parts for all of us," said Sonya. "I want the audience to come away with the message that looks aren't everything."

"Good." Satisfied that that was all taken care of, Terri charged ahead of the others so that she could be the first inside. Angela quickly followed but couldn't look at Terri without getting mad. Not only did Terri have to be the greatest gymnast in the world, she had to go after the greatest guy in the world.

Angela scanned the room for Bobby. Not there yet. Phew! She could dash into the rest room to comb her hair and put on some lip gloss.

Dawn came in and watched her. "Look, Angie, Bobby is just a member of the human race. You shouldn't go to any special trouble to look good for him."

Angela looked at Dawn's reflection in the mirror. "Oh, yeah? You think I'm a lost cause, huh?"

"No, silly. You look fine. But he should like you for just the way you are," Dawn advised.

"Thank you," replied Angela. She sighed. "He just happens to be special, and I want to look my best, especially with all those sharks out there who call themselves my friends.''

Dawn slid her fingers through her hair. ''Well, if you ask me, it's not worth it to make such a fuss over boys. They get conceited. We girls have to stick together.''

''Tell the sharks that,'' grumbled Angela.

The door swung open and Terri, Linda, and Sonya walked in.

''Speak of the devils,'' said Dawn. ''Or sharks.''

''Private conference time?'' Terri asked, raising her eyebrows.

''Oh, no, I have a pimple on my chin,'' groaned Sonya, leaning in to peer at herself in the mirror.

''Why don't you leave it alone? My mother always tells me not to pick them, or else they look like Mount Vesuvius,'' Dawn advised.

Sonya frowned at her. ''If it looks like Mount Vesuvius, you won't be able to see my face.''

''Could be an improvement,'' said Terri jokingly. Sonya threw her hairbrush at her. Terri dodged and it clattered to the tile floor.

When Angela stepped out of the rest room, Bobby walked in the door of the building. Her heart flip-flopped at the sight of him. He was wearing jeans and a Phantom of the Opera sweatshirt. He smiled at her, and she smiled back.

In the next second, however, Terri was zooming out of the rest room and waving at Bobby until Angela thought her arms would fall off. Bobby grinned. From behind Angela, Linda darted out and immediately launched a series of cartwheels across the floor, coming to a stop next to Terri. She was so obviously showing off! When she finished, Bobby walked up to Terri and her, ignoring Angela! Angela's heart sank like a stone.

"Hey, I really liked seeing you guys on TV," said Bobby. "You were both great."

"Thanks," chimed Terri and Linda, their faces beaming.

Angela wished their faces would crack.

"I just wanted to tell you that," he said, shuffling nervously from one foot to the other.

"Yeah, well, great," said Linda. "Glad you watched us."

"Hey, we have a gym meet a week from this coming Sunday. You can come if you want," suggested Terri.

Angela's mouth dropped open. Sonya came up next to her and stared at her.

"Close your mouth, Angie. A bug might fly in it," she whispered, pushing Angela's chin up.

Angela gave Terri a piercing glare, but Terri wouldn't meet her gaze. She was too busy staring at Bobby.

"Sure, sounds good. Where is it?" Bobby asked.

Terri told him where the meet would be held and how to get there. But then Ms. Bergman entered the room and said that they would be going up on the small stage at the far end of the large, open room later to begin work on the script she had given them in the last class.

"First, today, we're going to express our feelings," she announced. "I'm going to pair you off and then I'll ask you to express a particular emotion."

She matched couples around the room. Angela was staring off into space when Ms. Bergman called her name.

"Angela and Bobby will be a pair," she said. "And Terri and Dawn . . ."

Angela jumped to attention. Angela and Bobby? Her happiness didn't last long as she remembered how enthusiastic he'd been about Terri and Linda. She could only scowl. Out of the corner of her eye, Angela caught Bobby studying her thoughtfully.

"Angela? What's the matter?" he asked.

"What? Oh, nothing. Just practicing my emotions," she said.

"Express happiness," said Ms. Bergman. Everyone in the class smiled at one another.

Bobby reached for Angela's hand and squeezed it. "Angela, I'm so happy to see you," he said, grinning.

"Me, too. I mean, I'm happy to see me and you," she stammered, smiling. Then she thought, Oh, no, I hope he doesn't think I mean *me and you together*.

He kept holding her hand. Her hand was as damp as wilted lettuce. But it did feel nice to have her hand held.

Then Ms. Bergman said, "Okay, now be angry."

Angela looked into Bobby's eyes. She wasn't angry anymore and she didn't want to break the romantic spell. Bobby made a grumpy face and dropped her hand.

Angela remembered his ignoring her and greeting Terri and Linda instead. Immediately she recalled how her anger had felt. "I'm mad at you, Bobby," she told him.

"Oh, yeah? What did I do?" he demanded, shoving his hands in his pockets.

She couldn't tell him the truth. After all, this was only an acting assignment. But what could she say? Quick, make something up, she told herself. "Uh, you made my hands sweaty."

"You're blaming me for your sweat glands?" Bobby threw back his head and laughed.

Angela felt her skin grow hot. Other students turned around to watch them. It was turning into a ridiculous conversation. "Yes, I am."

"Okay, that's it, then. I'll never hold your hand again," he said, crossing his arms firmly over his chest.

Angela opened her mouth to say something, but just then Ms. Bergman said, "Now I want you to—show excitement!"

"That's great, just great!" exclaimed Angela. A big wad of tears pushed at the back of her throat, and she had to swallow hard to keep herself from crying.

Ms. Bergman came around to check on each couple. She stared at Angela and Bobby for a few moments.

"Angela, you're really very good. I can feel excitement traveling out from your body," Ms. Bergman said admiringly. "Your eyes are wide and glistening—wonderful."

Angela gulped and looked from Bobby to Ms. Bergman. The teacher didn't know she looked that way because she really was feeling all the emotions she had to act. "Thank you, Ms. Bergman."

"Hey, Angie, you could win an Academy Award for that performance," said Bobby, grinning.

Angela's heart pounded. He had called her *Angie* and mentioned the Academy Awards all in one sentence. She forgot about her sweaty hands. She was ready to burst with excitement. "Yeah," she stammered.

"Yeah."

Chapter Six

❀

On Thursday Angela was in science class, dreaming Bobby was stuck in quicksand and she was shoveling him out with a spoon. Meanwhile, Mr. Klein was lecturing on amoebas. Next to Angela, Howard Tarter was entertaining Sonya and a few others with his amoeba imitation. The girls had almost all their classes together this term.

"Howard, excuse me, but exactly what are you doing?" Mr. Klein asked.

Howard was slumped in his seat with his lips curled up, cross-eyed. He sat up suddenly. "Doing my amoeba imitation."

Mr. Klein sighed. "Well, you look like an amoeba with a fat lip."

The class burst out laughing.

"Thank you, Mr. Klein," said Howard, uncrossing his eyes.

"I suppose I can't say that you aren't contributing to the class, can I?" Mr. Klein said, then leafed through the textbook. "Okay, let's keep the horsing or 'amoebaing' to a minimum."

Angela was relieved that Howard's antics kept the teacher's attention off her. He might guess she was daydreaming, and she couldn't keep her mind on amoebas for anything. After all, amoebas were just blobs and Bobby was anything but blobby.

"There will be a test on this chapter Friday, class," announced Mr. Klein after the bell had rung.

"Ugh. Amoebas are the absolute worst," groaned Angela as they filed out of the classroom.

"I like Howard's amoeba the best," said Sonya, grinning.

"Yeah, Howard wins the Best Amoeba Award," quipped Angela.

Howard raced by on his way to his next class. "Hey, I'm sympathetic to the lowest forms of life. Now, don't forget the meeting during the last hour of school."

The girls laughed.

The talent show meeting attracted many more people than the earlier ones because kids got to get out of class to attend. Eddie Martin and Tommy Atwood came, plus some of the sixth graders who never got involved in anything. Even Celia showed up. Sonya and Howard announced the entries out loud. There were ballet and modern dance routines, singing and comedy acts, and skits.

"Eddie Martin and Tommy Atwood—The Three Stooges," read Howard. He stared at the two boys. "Hey, can't you guys count?"

"We're looking for another stooge," said Eddie seriously. "Any volunteers?"

Anna Camerini, a small, skinny sixth grader with braces, raised her hand.

"Sonya, Angela, Terri, Dawn, and Linda—a monster skit,

written by Sonya Plummer,'' announced Sonya, smiling. Her friends applauded.

"Well, that shouldn't be too hard for you guys," said Celia, smirking.

Sonya ignored the remark and read: "Celia, Polly, and Jeannie—a Gilbert and Sullivan surprise."

Howard whistled through his teeth. "Hurry up and submit a complete idea, Celia, so we know what we have to do."

"Howard—monologue—'A Day in the Life of a Hamster,' " Sonya continued.

"Okay, that's it. Now, I don't need anything for my monologue except a microphone and maybe a few lettuce leaves. What do you stooges need?" he asked Eddie, Tommy, and Anna.

"Chairs and a backdrop of some kind," suggested Eddie. "We'll probably bonk each other over the head with something like a rubber bottle."

"Okay. Sonya, what're you guys going to need?" asked Howard.

"Scary masks, a couple of surgical masks, and maybe surgical gowns," she said.

"We're not doing surgery in this, are we?" asked Terri.

"Well, there's the plastic surgery part," Sonya reminded her.

"Well, they all *need* plastic surgery," said Celia, loud enough for everyone to hear.

"You stay out of this," ordered Terri.

"I think we need an operating room and a beautiful garden," said Angela. "Maybe the masked people can think the garden is ugly and the trash bin is beautiful."

"Yuk," said Linda. "I don't like that."

"I don't like the operating room," said Dawn.

"You guys work this out somewhere else," suggested Howard. "Who's going to be the M.C.?"

"I think Angela should be the M.C.," offered Eddie.

"Not Angela. She'll have too much to do," said Terri. "How about Polly?"

"Polly's got too much to do," said Celia in her defense.

"Why not Angela?" questioned Dawn.

Angela jumped up. "May I speak for myself, please? Maybe I'd like to be the M.C.!"

"Why don't we vote?" suggested Howard.

"No, I think some person who doesn't have anything to do should be it," said Dawn.

"Who?" everyone chorused. There wasn't anyone at the meeting who wasn't involved in the show in some way.

"Okay, let's vote, then. All in favor of Angela, raise their hands—" ordered Howard. It turned out that Angela, Polly, and Dawn got the same number of votes. "Let's have all of you be the M.C.'s at different times. Now, let's arrange the order of the acts." Howard pushed his glasses up on his nose, looking flustered.

"I think we should open with something funny," suggested Angela.

"No, something serious," Sonya said.

"Something horrible," Terri put in loudly.

"Something dramatic," added Linda.

"I like the Three Stooges," offered Dawn. "I think they should go first."

"Something funny is best because it sets the tone for the rest of the show," explained Angela, feeling very proud of herself for making that sophisticated statement.

"Our skit isn't funny," Sonya announced.

"I thought our skit was supposed to be funny," said Angela.

"The only good skits are funny," Terri stated.

"That's not true! I want to do something meaningful!" cried Sonya. She rose from her seat and shook her fist.

"Well, go do it somewhere else!" yelled Terri. Her hair was standing straight up, as though she had just seen a ghost.

"Please, don't argue, you guys!" cried Dawn, who hated to see anyone fight.

"Sonya, if you can't hold this committee together, then I'll have to appoint somebody who can," Howard told her fiercely. "Maybe Linda could do it."

Linda beamed. Sometimes, Angela thought she had a secret crush on Howard.

Sonya scowled at Linda and then Howard. "That's not fair, Howard. I'm doing a good job. Everybody else is messing it up."

"No, you're not," Howard insisted.

"Yes, I am!"

"No!"

"Yes!"

Celia laughed as if she was better than everyone at the meeting. Then she, Polly, and Jeannie excused themselves in very loud voices. Other kids started to leave, too. Angela and Sonya exchanged worried looks. The meeting was ending up a total disaster.

Finally, even Dawn rose to leave. "Bye," she said hurriedly.

Angela, Terri, Linda, and Sonya rode to their acting class together, even though they were barely speaking to one another. Dawn arrived a few minutes later carrying a box of doughnuts from her parents' bakery, the Fresh Bakery.

"I thought everyone might like a snack," she said, handing the box to Angela to hold while she took off her jacket.

"Anything from your bakery's a treat," said Linda.

Dawn snatched the box back from Angela just as Sonya had her hand ready to plunge into the warm doughnuts.

Dawn walked directly across the room to where Bobby was standing and offered him a doughnut before offering them to anyone else—even Ms. Bergman.

"She's the last person on earth I would expect to do something like this," Angela said mournfully.

Bobby smiled at Dawn and took a big bite of a chocolate-covered doughnut. Dawn strolled back to her friends, her cheeks pink and her eyes lit up. "Bobby likes the doughnuts," she announced.

"We noticed," replied Angela. "But you're not supposed to like boys, Dawn."

"Well, I don't. Not really, that is," she said, her cheeks growing pink.

"You're the type of person I can trust, right? You wouldn't move in on someone else's territory, like *some* people I know." Angela looked meaningfully at Terri, Sonya, and Linda.

Terri, Sonya, and Linda dug into the box and started eating. Sonya soon had powdered sugar all over her lips.

"Well, sure. You know me," Dawn replied, smiling at them all. "Angela, what're you so upset about? I mean, I just offered Bobby a doughnut. I didn't ask him to marry me."

The girls laughed. Angela turned red. "I'm glad to hear that. It's such a relief," she said sarcastically.

Some girls went over and started talking to Bobby. He was surrounded by girls. All Angela could see of him was the top of his blond curly head. And Bobby was so good-looking, she thought he should be arrested for stopping traffic.

What kind of chance did she stand with the greatest guy in the world?

Chapter Seven

⚘

"There's never anything to eat here anymore, Angela," complained Terri as she stared at the plate of carrot and celery sticks, broccoli, and dip that Angela had placed in front of her.

Angela, Terri, Dawn, Linda, and Sonya were sitting in Angela's bedroom, draped over her wicker chairs.

"Yeah. Your house used to be the best for snacks," said Sonya.

"Health food never hurt anyone," said Angela, handing around diet sodas. "You'll live longer."

"Yeah, right. Whoever heard of anyone getting a heart attack in the sixth grade?" asked Linda.

"I think it could happen," said Dawn knowledgeably. Sonya glanced at her sideways.

"Okay, let's get down to business," said Terri, leaping to her feet. "I think we should each do what we do best in this skit, like Linda and I should do gymnastics."

"But that's not how the script goes," protested Sonya. "It's not about gymnastics."

"It would be great if we could put it in," Linda said. "People should see how great Terri and I are."

"I don't think it's a good idea," said Angela.

"I want to tap," said Dawn, crunching down on a carrot stick.

Sonya got up and handed everyone a copy of her script. "Look, read this and see what you think. I think Terri, Angela, and me should be the masked people, and Dawn and Linda can be the normal ones."

"I want to wear a mask," Dawn protested. "Look what I brought. They're my brother's." She pulled some rubber Halloween masks from a paper bag.

"You just don't want to be operated on," noted Terri, laughing.

"But I don't want to be a surgeon, either," Dawn complained.

"You should be a tap-dancing doctor, Dawn," said Terri, laughing.

"Look, are we going to do this skit, or aren't we?" demanded Angela, flapping her script in the air.

"Let me introduce you to the characters," said Sonya. She flopped down in one of the wicker chairs beneath a poster of the musical *Cats* and started reading out loud. " 'The Ugly-faces are obviously the ugly ones, and their names are: Globface and Hairface. The beautiful people are called Sweet-faces, and their names are: Moonface, Starface, and Sugar-face.' "

"Moonface makes me think of someone with acne," Angela pointed out.

"Let's change that one, then. How about Sunface?" Dawn suggested.

"Okay, let's start with my part," said Sonya. " 'The Uglyfaces are back in all their grossness. I get sick each time I see one.' ''

Angela interrupted her. "Why are you getting the biggest part? It looks like you have more to say than any of us, Sonya."

"Maybe because I know what I'm doing," she returned.

Terri rolled her eyes. "Oh, come on, Plummer! Give us a break."

"That's not fair, Sonya," Dawn insisted.

"Yeah," said Linda.

"Okay, I'll write more dialogue for you guys," Sonya replied reluctantly. "But just read your parts for now."

Angela looked down at her script. She was Sunface, one of the Sweetfaces. She decided to add a few gestures to her part, so she stood with a werewolf mask on, looking in the mirror, rearranging her hair. She read from the script:

" 'Maybe if we could change the Uglyfaces and make them look as good as we do, life would be much easier.' ''

" 'Then we'd be staring at them all the time. Like we stare at each other now,' '' Terri read.

" 'Yes, you are so beautiful. I can't get any work done because I keep staring at you, Starface,' '' said Sonya, staring at Terri.

Everyone laughed except Sonya, who frowned.

"Sonya, if we have to call each other names like Globface and Hairface, we won't be able to stop laughing," said Angela.

"It's supposed to be serious, though. Maybe I should change the names," she suggested.

"No, we like them, don't we, guys?" asked Linda, stifling a giggle.

"Yes, they're very original," said Terri. "My favorite is Hairface."

Dawn and Angela collapsed in a fit of giggles.

"All right, come on, we've got more to do!" cried Sonya, flouncing across the room. She tried on Angela's purple jean jacket and twirled around in it. "Let's get back to me not being able to get any work done."

Terri laughed. "Okay, Sugarface. Anything you say." She did a handstand.

Angela rolled her eyes. Dawn and Linda giggled.

" 'I think that the operation will be a success and we'll be able to make beautiful-looking people like us,' " read Angela, putting a Frankenstein mask up to her face.

The others burst into hysterics.

" 'Our ideal perfect person!' " cried Sonya, clapping her hands together.

Linda vaulted off the bed and read to Dawn: " 'I heard them talking about changing us, Globface.' "

Dawn giggled. " 'Oh, no! I like me the way I am. I don't want to look like them.' "

Angela, Terri, and Sonya descended on Dawn and Linda wearing the dimestore masks. Everyone piled on top of one another and dissolved in shrieks of laughter.

" 'But we're so beautiful!' " cried Terri, rubbing her mask face against Dawn's arm like a cat.

"Ouch, it's scratchy. Get away from me!" yelled Dawn, rubbing her arm.

"It's just rubber," said Terri.

"I still think we should do a gym routine with the masks on," said Linda, clambering out from under everybody. "It would make it more interesting."

"And everyone would look at you and Terri instead of the rest of us," Sonya pointed out.

"Well, what's wrong with that?" demanded Terri.

Angela stuck her hands on her hips. "It just so happens

that we're in this together. You are really great gymnasts, but you are not the only ones in it.''

"You sound jealous," Terri said, pirouetting out the door. The others followed her outside to their bikes.

Angela was relieved when her friends had gone. Usually, she loved having them all over, but that day they tired her out with all their arguing. Plus, she had to study. But as she opened her book, she wondered, who did Bobby *really* like?

Chapter Eight

⌘

"Oh, look, Angie! There's that old bicycle built for two we always planned to fix up," cried Mrs. King, wheeling an old rusty bike out from a corner of the basement.

Angela and her mother were spending part of Saturday cleaning out the basement so that they could put new stuff in that they could throw out the next year.

"Let me see," said Angela, taking the bike from her mother. "Does it still work?"

Angela checked the tires, which obviously needed air, and the brakes, which were rusted stiff. "Maybe we could really get it fixed up now. Wouldn't it be fun?"

"Yes. I'll be glad to pay for it, honey. How romantic," Mrs. King sighed, stopping what she was doing.

"Mom, since when did you decide rusty bikes are romantic?" asked Angela. Her mother was usually down-to-earth about everything except food.

Mrs. King blushed prettily. "Oh, well, I guess since Ross Bugrin asked me out."

"You're kidding!" exclaimed Angela, nearly dropping the bike on her toes.

"No, I'm not. Isn't it nice?" Mrs. King smiled.

"Great," said Angela, but she wasn't all that sure she was glad. After all, if Bobby's father was taking her mother out, it would be really weird if Angela and Bobby were having a romance, too. She decided not to think about it.

"Oh, and do you know what Ross told me? He said that Bobby won baby contests. He sometimes models for magazines even now," Mrs. King went on.

"Really?" Angela felt annoyed that her mother knew this interesting fact about Bobby before she did.

"Yes. He is cute, but I didn't know he modeled."

Angela had an idea. She would get the bike fixed, and ask Bobby if he wanted to go for a ride on it. She figured he'd jump at the chance to ride a bicycle built for two.

"Mom, how much longer do we have to work down here?" Angela asked.

"Let's call it a day," said Mrs. King, dusting off her hands. "Come on, let's change."

After they cleaned up, Mrs. King drove Angela to a bike shop. The repairwoman, Sally, said she could fix the bike by Wednesday. Angela decided that next Thursday, during acting class, she'd ask Bobby about going bike riding. If all her friends could go after Bobby, she decided, so could she.

On Thursday before acting class began, Angela watched Bobby out of the corner of her eye to see which one of her friends he seemed to like the best. She counted the times he looked at each of them: he didn't look at Dawn at all, Terri twice, Sonya twice, and Linda didn't count because she went right up to him and flirted directly with him. Angela was annoyed and decided to act. Before Ms. Bergman came in, she strode right up to him.

"Hi, Bobby," she said, smiling.

She heard one of her friends behind her gasp. She thought it sounded like Dawn's gasp.

"Hi, Angela," he said.

"You'll never guess what I found in our basement while we were cleaning it out," she said.

"A skeleton?" he asked jokingly.

"No, a bicycle built for two," she told him.

"Is it an antique?" he asked.

"Well, I guess so. It's really old," replied Angela. "Anyway, I was wondering if maybe you wanted to go for a ride on it sometime."

"Oh, yeah, great. I've never ridden on one of those. That would be really fun," he said, smiling at her.

Angela thought she'd melt. "How about Saturday?" she asked him.

"Saturday sounds great," he replied, grinning.

She nearly floated back to her friends.

"What was all that about?" demanded Sonya, frowning.

Angela sighed dreamily. "We're going bike riding Saturday."

"Wow! A real date?" exclaimed Dawn.

Angela turned bright red and looked around to see if Bobby had heard Dawn. He saw her looking at him and waved, and Angela waved back. "Shhh," she said to Dawn, putting a finger over her lips.

"Keep quiet, pinhead," ordered Terri. "No need to make a public announcement."

Ms. Bergman called the class to order. Their lesson that day was to read a passage from Shakespeare. " 'To be or not to be, that is the question,' " recited Ms. Bergman in her rich stage voice. "I'm sure you've all heard that before."

"Wow, I want to do Shakespeare," said Angela enthusiastically.

"There are many modern stories that have been taken from Shakespeare," said Ms. Bergman. "Can anyone name one?"

Angela raised her hand. "*West Side Story* was taken from *Romeo and Juliet,*" she said. "It's the story of a boy and girl whose families don't approve of their romance, but in *West Side Story,* the kids are part of rival street gangs, which are sort of like families."

"It doesn't sound like the same story to me," argued Terri.

"It's a perfect example of what I'm talking about," said Ms. Bergman. "And we can find other stories that seem related to Shakespearean stories. The settings change from castles to condominiums, the characters might be modern instead of medieval, but the story itself is often basically the same."

Angela gave Terri a smug look. Terri stuck her tongue out at her. Ms. Bergman had them read passages from Shakespeare until they could do it almost naturally. They emerged from class speaking like people from Shakespeare's time.

"I didn't know you knew all that about Shakespeare," Linda commented.

"I hath been studying," replied Angela with pride.

"Hey, what you said about Shakespeare was great, Angela," said Bobby, coming up behind the girls. "He's really cool."

"Was," corrected Angela.

"Yeah, but you kind of think of him as being still alive," said Bobby, walking beside her. "I guess it's the words."

"It must be the slang he uses," said Terri, laughing.

"I think Shakespeare is romantic," said Sonya, sighing deeply and gazing longingly at Bobby.

Angela shot her a look of pure hatred.

On Saturday Angela spent about half an hour looking at herself in the mirror. Finally she decided to tie her hair up in a big flowered ribbon before she set off on her ride to Bobby's.

He was outside when she arrived, working with three pieces of plastic tubing with a loop of fabric cord attached and a large bucket.

"What's that?" Angela asked when she approached him.

Bobby was on his knees, dipping the device into a bucket. "It's a super soap-bubble blower. See—I'm dipping it into soapy water. Let's see how it works."

He held the bubble blower up in front of him and flicked his wrists gently. A bubble the size of a beach ball emerged and shimmered for a minute before being blown away on the sea wind.

"That's neat," said Angela as Bobby made another one. Then he let her try it.

Bobby said, "Hey, there are bicycle paths along the cliffs. We can ride along there, if you want."

"Sure."

Angela got on the front and Bobby climbed on behind her. He was taller than she, so he got some tools from the garage and adjusted the seat to his height.

They rode along the cliff, watching people sunbathe and collect driftwood on the beach. It was a breezy day, but the sun was bright. Angela liked the way the combination of wind and sun felt against her bare arms. She liked feeling Bobby's steady weight on the back of her bike, and hearing his pedaling in rhythm with her own.

They stopped at a hot dog stand, even though Angela said she didn't eat hot dogs. They weren't part of her diet plan.

"Angie, just because you don't eat hot dogs, you don't have to be a smarty about it," said Bobby, shoving a hot dog at her.

"I'm on a special diet," she told him.

"You're skinny," he said, looking her up and down as though trying to find a lump of fat on her.

"Thanks, and I want to stay that way." She ate a hot dog but without the bun.

She frowned at him. "If I did that, I'd be a blimp."

Before her eyes, he demolished french fries, an ice-cream sundae, salad, three hot dogs, and a milk shake.

"I can't believe anyone can eat that much," she told him. It wasn't such a long time ago that Angela had eaten almost that much. But Bobby could do it without gaining weight. Bobby could probably eat an entire banquet dinner and not get fat.

"I should enter one of those watermelon-eating contests," said Bobby, grinning at her.

"Did you really win baby contests?" asked Angela.

Bobby started laughing. "I can tell my dad's been bragging again. Yes, I did, but I think I'd rather be in a watermelon-eating contest than a beauty contest."

They locked up the bike and walked down on the beach. Bobby began to make a sand castle, and they pretended to be the king and queen of the castle.

"I want six white horses to fill the stables," said Bobby.

"Well, you'd better make a lot of money," Angela told him, laughing. "I want a moat," she declared. "Make me a moat, King."

"Yes, Your Highnie, anything you say," he replied, and they collapsed in a fit of giggles.

The tide bubbled up and turned their castle into a blob. Angela got all wet, but she didn't mind. Bobby was so funny, pretending to be the king of the blobby castle. Angela hated to think this, but maybe being with Bobby was more fun than being with her friends.

Chapter Nine

⌗

Sunday was the day of Linda and Terri's gymnastics meet. Angela, Sonya, and Dawn met Linda and Terri at Terri's house, and waited while the two girls pulled on their red- and blue-striped leotards and tights.

The first thing Terri asked Angela was "How was our Bobby yesterday?" in a sarcastic voice.

Angela decided to make the most of it. "He was great—perfect. We rode my bike all day, ate hot dogs, and built a sand castle—"

"Angela, have I got this right?" asked Terri. "You don't eat hot dogs anymore and you hate sand."

"Well, I didn't eat the hot dog bun, and I didn't notice the sand until later, after I got home and washed my hair," Angela explained. Somehow, the sand hadn't mattered while she was with Bobby.

"I think you've gone crazy," said Terri.

"He's just a boy," reminded Dawn.

"Maybe, but you like him, too," Angela pointed out.

Dawn blushed. "Well, he's a *cute* boy."

In one movement Terri hitched her leotard up on her shoulders. Her arms were as skinny as twigs, thought Angela.

"You're sure taking a long time to get ready, Linda," noted Angela. Linda had been applying lip gloss and brushing her golden blond hair until it shone.

"I have to look really super," she replied, and pulled her hair back into a ponytail.

Linda was pretty and very sly and clever. You never quite knew what she was thinking, Angela thought.

The girls wouldn't all fit in Terri's parents' car so they went to the meet on their bikes. Celia was already there, warming up. She looked super as usual with a red velvet ribbon tying back her hair.

Angela, Sonya, and Dawn got seats in the third row to root for their friends. Terri was by far the most expert gymnast of the group, with Celia coming in a close second.

Terri's floor routine was a series of quickly executed leaps and turns that left the audience breathless. Celia's routine was slower and more elegant, but without any of the fancy footwork that Terri used.

The audience stood and applauded when the performance was over. That was when Angela saw Bobby. He was standing two rows in front of her. As soon as the clapping stopped he moved onto the gym floor to talk to Terri.

"Great performance," he told Terri, grinning.

Terri grinned back at him.

Linda was standing next to her, her blond hair still perfectly in place. Linda didn't even seem to sweat.

"Hi, Bobby," she said, greeting him.

At that moment Celia noticed Bobby and pushed toward him past all her friends. "Who is this?" she asked Linda.

"None of your business!" declared Terri. Then, as if they

had planned it, Dawn circled around Bobby and crowded Celia out.

Luckily, Polly dragged Celia away just then to talk to her parents.

Dawn and Sonya watched Bobby and Angela together, while Terri and Linda ran backstage to change.

Bobby blushed and smiled at Angela. "Hi, how are you?" he asked.

"Fine," she said. "I didn't remember you'd be here."

"It was a great show, wasn't it?" he asked.

"Yes, it was great, really great," Angela replied, swallowing hard. "My friends are really—very talented and great." She felt as if she were going to cry and didn't want him to see her so she turned away.

"Angela, are you okay?" he asked.

"Sure," she replied in a muffled tone, facing a blank wall so he couldn't see her tears.

Terri came up just then and lightly punched her forearm. "Hey, Angie, let's go get a pizza and celebrate, okay?"

"I'm not in the mood," Angela replied.

"Aw, come on, we have to celebrate," urged Sonya.

"No, I don't feel well all of a sudden. In fact, I feel awful," she said. With that, Angela pushed past her friends, tramped over the exercise mats, and ran outside to the bike racks.

Now she knew why Linda had made such a big deal about looking nice. It was because of Bobby. And even though she knew the girls had invited Bobby to the meet, she knew they hadn't given him all the details, such as the time and place. That meant Terri or Linda had to have called him. How could they call themselves "friends" after doing something like this? she wondered, wiping hot tears from her cheeks with the back of her hand.

* * *

"Oh, Angie darling, did I tell you that Bobby and his father are coming to dinner tomorrow night?" said Mrs. King as she pushed white dough through a pasta maker before breakfast on Monday morning.

"Oh, Mom," groaned Angela. "Do they have to?"

"No, they don't have to, but I want them to," replied Mrs. King happily. "We'll have pasta. Let's see, how about clam sauce?"

"Not clam sauce, Mom. It's so messy!" exclaimed Angela.

"We'll all be messy, so it'll be okay," Mrs. King said as she hung the pasta up to dry.

Angela had a vision of herself sitting there with sauce slowly staining her chin and shirt.

As the girls were riding to school that same morning, they noticed how quiet Angela was. "What's up, Angie? Cat got your tongue?" asked Linda.

"She's mad because Bobby came to the meet yesterday," supplied Terri.

"It's not that," said Angela, riding next to Linda. "Bobby and his father are coming to our house for dinner tomorrow night."

"Wow, lucky you!" cried Linda. "I wish my mom would invite them for dinner."

"Your mother is married, remember?" said Angela.

"Oh, yeah, I forgot." She giggled.

"Look. It's different when your mom starts inviting your possible boyfriend over, and his father is her possible boyfriend. I mean, they've already gone out on a date," said Angela.

"That's tough," said Dawn sympathetically. "That sort of makes him part of your family. What're you going to do?"

Angela shrugged. "I don't know. What am I going to wear?"

"We'll think of something, don't worry," said Sonya. Clothes were one of her favorite subjects.

Angela gazed at her in surprise. "You're going to help me, even though this is for Bobby?"

Sonya shrugged. "Sure, why not? You're my friend, aren't you? He doesn't have anything to do with us being friends."

That was one thing that was good about her friends, thought Angela. Even though they might be mad at one another, they usually could manage to forget their differences if one of them needed help with a problem.

After school Sonya and Dawn came over to help Angela with her wardrobe. They pulled nearly everything out of her closet and laid it on the bed.

"Okay, I like these three outfits," said Sonya, pointing to a green pants outfit, a blue jeans outfit, and a polka dot dress.

"Maybe I can wear all three—you know, make quick changes," suggested Angela.

"He'd think you were crazy," said Sonya, shaking her head. "I think the polka dots are nice."

"Yeah, they're kind of fun," said Angela thoughtfully. She decided to wear the dress.

Angela ran to answer the door the next night when Bobby and his father arrived. Bobby looked handsome in a navy crewneck sweater, light blue sports shirt, and brown cords. His usually tousled hair had been slicked down with water.

"What's for dinner?" asked Mr. Bugrin, stepping inside the door and flaring his nostrils to smell in an exaggerated way. "I smell something super."

"Oh, just something Mom cooked up," said Angela shyly. Bobby was so close to her she could feel his warm breath on her cheek.

"I brought some games," he said, pulling out two travel board games from a plastic bag.

"Bobby thought we were going on vacation instead of out to dinner," said Mr. Bugrin jovially. "I told him you probably had a Scrabble game or two."

"We do, yes, but that's okay," said Angela.

Mrs. King walked in then and took over. "Oh, Ross, it's so nice to see you. And Bobby, how are you?" she said, extending a hand to each of them.

Mrs. King wore a bright fuchsia dress that made her look like a walking plum. Angela thought her mom looked weird, but Mr. Bugrin and Bobby seemed to like her just fine.

Angela and Bobby drank soda and played a game in the living room while their parents were in the kitchen, putting the finishing touches on dinner.

"Dinner's ready," called Mrs. King finally as she carried a steaming platter to the table.

"Looks and smells wonderful, Ellen," said Mr. Bugrin, seating her. "Everyone's envious of me, being invited to your house for dinner."

Mrs. King turned red. Angela didn't know whether her mom was blushing or just flushed with heat from cooking.

"Well, tuck in your bibs!" she ordered.

Angela took tiny bites of the sauce to avoid getting all messy. Of course, the pasta sauce was dreamy. Usually, she wore her napkin tucked into the neck of her shirt for this meal.

Bobby didn't seem to care, and began eating right away, letting the sauce dribble down his chin.

Mr. Bugrin twirled pasta around his fork. "Ellen, this is

great first-time-eating-together food," he said jokingly. "You invite someone to dinner and watch them struggle not to make a mess."

"A little sauce on the face never hurt anyone," said Mrs. King.

After dinner Angela and Bobby did the dishes while the adults looked at family pictures. Then Angela took Bobby into her room to listen to records. She had cleaned her room especially because he was coming over.

Angela's walls were decorated with Broadway posters.

"Hey, cool," said Bobby as he admired the room. "Where'd you get such great posters?"

"At Poster Heaven, in town," she told him. "Some had to be ordered especially from New York."

"Wow. I like the same stuff, you know," he said.

She put on a sound track of a popular musical, which filled the small room.

"Now, how did you know I loved that?" he said, flopping back in one of her wicker chairs.

She shrugged. "It's my favorite."

"We like a lot of the same things," he said. "How about Scrabble?"

"Sure. But watch out. I'm a hot Scrabble player," she warned him.

He laughed. He opened up his small Scrabble set and Angela told him about the skit they were doing at school.

"I can lend you a mask if you like," he said, spreading out the letter tiles.

"Oh, that'd be neat," said Angela.

"You can come over and pick out what you need," he told her.

Angela had just about forgotten she was mad about the gymnastics meet. This was much better, being invited to Bobby's to look at masks. What would her friends say about that? So far, they had done all the inviting, but Bobby had invited only her to his house.

When it was time to leave, Angela lent Bobby one of her albums.

"Okay, so Saturday you'll come over for the mask?" he asked her.

"Sounds good," she said. She felt her face grow warm.

As she watched Bobby and his father drive off, she thought, wow, this means I get to see Bobby again—and not just at acting class!

Chapter Ten

🞧

In the lunchroom at school the next day, Angela and her friends were discussing what they'd need for the talent show.

"We need masks and some kind of costumes," said Dawn.

"We can wear choir robes," suggested Linda. "We've got some in the basement of our house."

"Wow, choir robes would be great for the masked people," said Angela. "Bobby's got a mask collection and he's lending me one."

The others stood and gaped at her.

"Oh, yeah?" said Terri, scratching her spiky hair. "Since when?"

"Since he came to dinner at my house last night," Angela replied smugly.

"You didn't think about your friends needing masks. I guess," Linda observed.

"Listen, he offered me one. I didn't want to be greedy." Sometimes they made her so mad.

Terri sighed and took a big bite of her tunafish sandwich. "After all we've done for you, Angie," she said.

"Like trying to steal away my boyfriend?" she asked.

All of them started yelling at once. Ms. Dorrity, the lunch duty teacher, had to split them up—in front of the entire sixth grade. It was one of the few times that Angela wished she had never met them.

After school Angela and her friends hopped on their bikes and rode downtown. They went to a novelty shop that sold a variety of masks and other items.

"I don't think we need much," said Angela.

"We can use a bread knife or a letter opener for a scalpel," said Terri.

"Wow, I'm glad you're not my doctor," said Dawn, giggling.

They found surgical masks and tried them on. Then Angela discovered the scary masks, one with bloody mangled faces and eyes sliding off them. They chose a blue one for Starface and a wormy white one for Sugarface.

"We'll look great!" cried Sonya enthusiastically.

"Perfect!" said Terri, hidden behind the horrible blue mask. "Now let's see how they look with our choir robes.

They rode over to Linda's to check out the robes. Linda's house was pretty run-down. The house was in desperate need of a coat of paint and the front porch sagged. Her family didn't have a lot of money to fix it up.

Cobwebs tickled Angela's face as she descended the rickety staircase to the musty basement. Linda led the way, aiming a flashlight into the dark.

"Oh, here they are," she said, lifting up heavy lumps of fabric. She handed a robe to each of the girls.

"They smell like mothballs and dust," said Angela, wrinkling her nose.

"Well, they've been here since before we came," said

Linda. "I don't know who lived here before us. Maybe a whole choir."

The others laughed. They took the robes upstairs into the light and tried them on. With the masks, they looked as if they had just walked out of a horror movie.

"Maybe we should get the robes cleaned or something," suggested Dawn, who kept sneezing.

"Oh, why bother? They look great with all the dust and cobwebs on them," said Terri. "Really authentic." She patted her robe, and a cloud of dust rose into the air.

Angela took off her robe and Linda put all the robes in a pile. Then they went to her room and played around with makeup.

Linda's room was a clutter of makeup and discarded clothes. She almost never hung anything up, and nobody ever seemed to make her clean her room. Angela thought it was kind of cool.

"I think the two ugly people, Dawn and Linda, should look a little spacey," said Angela. "With really exaggerated makeup. Eyeliner out to their ears, maybe."

"Hey, sort of punky," said Dawn excitedly. "My sister Mariel could help us with that."

Sonya cringed. "I don't think we want to look that spacey, Dawn."

Mariel wore her light blond hair cropped really short, dyed it various colors, and sometimes wore a ring in her nose. It was sometimes hard to recognize her because she was always changing her appearance.

"Well, still, she can help us with makeup," Dawn said. She felt that Mariel was the most creative member of her family.

Sonya suddenly glanced at her watch and jumped from the floor, dropping an eyebrow pencil. "I've got to go. I promised Bobby I'd take him horseback riding. He's meeting me at my house in fifteen minutes.''

"What?'' Angela screeched. She had just outlined her lips with purple lipstick. Her hand jerked and she made a broad purple line across one cheek.

"You heard me,'' said Sonya, swinging her brown hair behind her ears. She started to leave the bedroom.

"How could you do this?'' cried Terri, glaring at Sonya.

"Well, it's a free country, you guys,'' Sonya replied defensively. "I can do what I want.''

"You didn't tell us about this, and we made these plans,'' insisted Angela. "And besides, Bobby likes me.''

"How do you know he likes only you?'' demanded Linda. "He might like all of us.''

"Yeah, did you ever think of that?'' asked Sonya.

"He can't like all of us,'' insisted Angela. "We're all so different. Anyway, you asked him behind our backs, Sonya.''

"No, I just forgot to mention it,'' Sonya replied, walking away.

"It's not just forgetting,'' Dawn said knowingly. "You did it on purpose.''

"I did not!'' cried Sonya. "And what do you care, you don't like boys.''

"I *do* like boys!'' Dawn told her, making a face.

"What's wrong with everybody around here?'' asked Terri.

"Yeah, I can't even ask Bobby to go riding without you all making a big stink,'' said Sonya.

"That's not true,'' Angela replied. "It was the way you did it that stinks.''

Sonya glared at her. "You know, Angie, you're the one causing all the problems with Bobby. He's just a regular guy, but you're making such a big deal about him that it messes us all up.''

"That's not true!" cried Angela. "If you cared about our friendship, you would never have asked him to go riding with you."

"You're crazy," said Sonya.

All the girls followed Sonya outside.

"Angie's right," said Dawn loyally. "It wasn't nice to do that."

"Yeah, Sonya. It's not friendly," added Linda.

"Just because I invited Bobby to go riding doesn't mean I don't like you guys anymore," Sonya insisted.

She climbed on her bike and rode down the driveway.

"Sometimes you're really a creep, Sonya!" yelled Angela.

"Sonya Plummer, we're never going to speak to you again," Terri said flatly.

"Yeah!" Angela and the others yelled after Sonya. But Sonya didn't stop, she just waved and acted as if she didn't care about what they said.

The next day at school Howard was mad at Sonya because he found out from Polly, who overheard Dawn talking to Angela in the hall, that Sonya had gone horseback riding with Bobby. Angela, Dawn, Terri, and Linda were still angry at her, too.

"You can't be a chairperson anymore," Howard announced at the talent show meeting held during last period.

"And why not?" demanding Sonya hotly.

"Because you're not doing your job," replied Howard. "Your best friends aren't even speaking to you."

"That's because they're jealous of me," she insisted.

Angela thought it was probably Howard who was jealous of Bobby, even though he didn't even know him.

"Linda, why don't you be chairperson?" Howard asked.

Linda grinned. "Oh, I'd love to," she answered.

"That's not fair!" cried Sonya, thumping her fist down on the desk.

"I think you're discriminating against Sonya because she went riding with—" Dawn stopped herself in midsentence. She blushed.

"Yeah, you can't take her off the job just because she went riding with another man," said Terri bluntly.

Celia's eyes lit up. "What other man?"

"Who said I was doing that?" cried Howard. "I'm doing it because she'd doing a lousy job of organizing. I'm the president here, and I get to decide what's going to happen."

Sonya glared at him, then she turned to Linda. "I don't know why you're so eager to take this job, Linda. You're supposed to be my friend."

"I *am* your friend," insisted Linda. It was the first time one of the friends had ever spoken directly to Sonya in twenty-four hours. "But somebody has to head the committee. Wouldn't you rather have me?"

"I'd rather have me," replied Sonya flatly.

"Can we get some work done?" asked Angela, brushing her dark hair away from her face.

"Yes!" Howard exclaimed. "We need to break down responsibilities even further. Now that Tommy has designed the sets, we need someone to paint them and do the lighting and props."

"I'll do it. I'm good at that stuff," offered Eddie Martin.

Ms. Kerry poked her head in the room to see how they were doing. "Celia, it's time to tell them what your act is," she urged.

"Ms. Kerry, I don't want anyone to know," said Celia. "Besides, Angela, Sonya, Dawn, Linda, and Terri are more of a problem than I am. They're always fighting about the talent show and boys and they're so-o-o disorganized."

Angela rolled her eyes. "We're not disorganized, Ms. Kerry."

"Yeah. We're fine," agreed Sonya, shooting a warning look at Howard which meant, Keep your mouth shut.

Ms. Kerry gritted her teeth. "Girls, I am so tired of your scrabbling. Please be aware of that, and work out your differences. Now!" she added very forcefully.

The advisor disappeared.

"I think she means it," said Angela to the other stunned onlookers.

Chapter Eleven

⌘

Angela rose her bike over to Bobby's house on Saturday. It was windy and waves were crashing against the rocks below the house. Angela knocked at the door and Bobby answered it.

He looked at her, grinning. "Hi, come in." She followed him into the house, which was decorated with wind chimes, shells, and bits of colored sea-tumbled glass.

"I like this house," said Angela, looking around her.

"It used to be owned by an old sea captain. My mom always thought there was a ghost living here," he told her, leading the way to his room. "My dad went down to the office for a couple of hours. But come and see my masks."

Bobby opened his bedroom door and then his closet door. Dozens of gross faces stared out at Angela from the closet shelves. She gasped when she saw them all.

"Wow. Where'd you get all those?" she asked.

He shrugged. "I buy them at flea markets. I fix broken ones, once I even found one in the garbage after Halloween."

"I love them," exclaimed Angela.

"You're supposed to hate them," Bobby told her, laughing.

"I like scary things," she replied.

He took one of the dark, bloody masks off the shelf. "How's this one for your skit?"

She held it up to her face and made her hands into a pair of claws.

He shrieked and held up his hands. "It looks great on you."

"Thanks." She giggled and tried on another one, yellow with eyeballs hanging down on long strings. "I like this one."

"You look like Miss America," he said. "Take it."

She stuffed it in her backpack.

"Now, how about some archery? We can go to the park nearby," he suggested.

"Oh, sure."

They went outside. He slung his bow and quiver full of arrows over his shoulder, and they climbed on their bikes. Bobby led the way to the archery range.

The target was tacked onto a wooden stand. It was designed with colored, numbered rings going into the center bull's-eye from one to ten.

"Whatever ring you hit, you earn the number of points in that ring. So if you hit the bull's-eye, you earn ten points," explained Bobby. He showed Angela how to hold the bow, nock an arrow, and place the arrow so that she could get a clear shot.

Angela liked her lesson because Bobby had to put his arms around her to teach her to shoot.

"Okay, try now," said Bobby, standing behind her.

She aimed and shot the arrow straight. It hit the bull's-eye with a *thunk!*

"Wow! Angie, look what you did! Congratulations!" he cried, slapping her on the back.

"Pretty good, huh?" She grinned at him.

"Yeah. Let's see if you can do it again," said Bobby, a challenging gleam in his eye.

Angela aimed again and shot a seven. Bobby looked at her approvingly.

"You're a good shot, Angie," he told her. "Another one of your talents."

She smiled and handed the bow to him. He scored an eight and six.

"I like this game," said Angela.

"Well, you can come over and shoot with me anytime," he told her.

"Well, if it isn't *Angela*," said a familiar, snotty voice.

Angela looked away from the target to see Celia, Polly, and Jeannie straddling their bikes while staring at her.

"What're you doing here?" she asked.

"Just riding," said Celia. "Does your mother know you're here?"

Angela felt her cheeks grow hot. "It's none of your business, Celia Forester!"

Bobby nocked another arrow and aimed; Angela hoped he hadn't heard her. The arrow made a *thunk* when it hit the target.

"Who're your friends?" he asked, lowering his bow and turning to Angela.

"Nobody you'd want to know," Angela replied.

He gave her a funny look. "Oh, why?"

"Because," replied Angela, frowning at Celia. The last thing she needed was for Bobby to like Celia.

"My name's Celia Forester," Celia told him, smiling triumphantly. "I saw you at the gymnastics meet." She pushed off and started to pedal away, looking straight at Bobby over her shoulder. Celia and her friends giggled and rode down a cement path.

Bobby waved, but Angela just stood still, her arms crossed. She felt very grumpy.

By the time Angela got to school on Monday morning, the entire school knew about her archery lesson.

"Angela, you and Bobby are hot news around here," said Terri, who, as usual, was one of the first people in the building.

"Who's the gossip?" asked Angela.

"Who else? Celia," replied Dawn. "She saw you at the park with Bobby, remember?"

"She thinks Bobby's cute, and wants to find out who he is," said Linda. "But we're not telling her."

"After the other day when I took him riding, I thought Bobby liked me," said Sonya. "But now I think he likes you, Angie, because *he* asked *you* to go shooting."

"Maybe he likes all of us," suggested Linda. "Maybe he's like one of those guys who has a bunch of wives."

"Linda, we're only in the sixth grade!" exclaimed Dawn.

Just then the bell rang, and the girls trooped off to homeroom. Angela was glad. Every time the conversation turned to boys or Bobby, they got into an argument.

Acting class was canceled that afternoon and the girls decided to rehearse at school. Celia dropped in and started pumping Angela for information about Bobby.

"So how did you meet this cute guy, Angela?" she asked.

"None of your business," replied Angela in a monotone.

"Who is he?" she persisted.

"No one," Angela told her.

"You're not being very cooperative," said Celia huffily. "I'll have to find out some other way, I guess."

"Do a few interviews, Celia," suggested Terri, laughing at her.

"But none of you will tell me anything," said Celia. "You're all in this together, I know you are. But what I can't figure out is why you're arguing."

The five friends laughed. For the next five seconds, they were "in it together" before they started to fight again.

Dawn had been painting some pictures of animals in gardens on large pieces of cardboard and started to show them off proudly.

"Uh, Dawn, they're nice, but they don't have anything to do with our skit," Sonya pointed out.

"Yeah, we don't have animals in the skit," added Angela.

"Yes, but we can write them in. You said yourself we could put anything in the skit that we wanted," insisted Dawn.

"But animals? We were talking about tap dancing and gymnastics and stuff," said Sonya.

"Maybe acrobatic animals?" suggested Howard.

"I don't think that's very funny," said Dawn seriously. She picked a rubber chicken out of one of the boxes. "I think animals would be cute in this thing."

"I don't want them," said Sonya. "I want scenes of rooms."

"Rooms are boring," said Dawn.

"I don't like the mask you have picked out, Angela," said Linda, joining in with all the protestors. "It's just too gross for the beautiful people."

"Well, that's tough. I want to use it," retorted Angela. "I want the beautiful people to be as ugly as possible."

"Then you don't really need masks," said Celia, snickering.

"Very funny," said Terri.

"Let's go over this one scene," suggested Sonya, paging through her script.

"I don't want to do the scene," announced Linda.

"Linda, will you just do what I want?" yelled Sonya. Exasperated, she threw a shawl at Linda. It landed on Linda's face, and she threw it straight back at Sonya.

"Sonya, that's not very nice!" yelled Dawn. She threw a rubber chicken straight at Sonya, but Sonya ducked and it missed her.

"I'd like to stuff this script in your mouth," said Linda, rolling up her copy.

Sonya turned bright red and wrung both ends of the shawl. "And I'd like to strangle you."

Terri threw an old shoe into the middle of the stage. Linda threw her script down so that the pages scattered. The stage was now littered with a rubber chicken, shawl, script pages, and a shoe.

"Girls! You're driving me nuts!" exclaimed Howard. "Stop it. Now, on with the show!"

They all started shouting at once. Ms. Kerry arrived on the scene.

"Okay, what's going on here? Why the mess?" she demanded.

"Dawn, Sonya, Angela, Linda, and Terri started throwing things, Ms. Kerry," said Celia, smiling at the teacher.

Ms. Kerry looked as if steam were ready to erupt from the top of her head. "This is your last warning. If you don't get your act together, I will assign you separate projects, or I will kick you out of this show. Do you understand? We will not have the show spoiled by this kind of behavior!"

Ms. Kerry's voice echoed throughout the auditorium. Angela shivered. She knew Ms. Kerry meant business, and she was scared.

What if the Spring Fling was a complete flop? What if they didn't get to be in it?

If it wasn't for Bobby, she knew they wouldn't be fighting. After all, this had never happened before.

The rest of the rehearsal went quietly, but not great. When it was over, Angela asked her friends to come over to her house.

"It's an emergency," she said.

They biked to her house in silence, because they were still pretty mad at one another. Angela brought some natural potato chips and diet soda into her bedroom and sat down in front of her friends.

"Look, if we don't do as Ms. Kerry says, we can get kicked out of the show," she said mournfully. "How many of us want that to happen?"

Everyone shook her head and stared at the carpet.

"I've decided what to do," she told them.

Terri, Sonya, Dawn, and Linda raised their eyes.

"I'm not going to like Bobby anymore," she announced.

"Just like that?" questioned Sonya. "Like you're a human faucet or something, turning off your feelings?"

"Sure. People break up all the time for good causes," said Angela. "And this is a good cause. Our friendship and our skit are at stake."

"But you and Bobby were never really going together," Terri pointed out.

Sonya was silent for a long time, then she said, "Well, if you don't like Bobby anymore, you don't mind if I still like him, do you?"

Angela's mouth fell open.

"I still like him, too," admitted Dawn. "But I don't think

we should spend a lot of time worrying about a boy. We're more important.''

"I don't think us not liking him anymore is going to help," said Linda.

Angela glared at Sonya, Linda, and Dawn. "You guys are traitors."

"We are not," protested Dawn.

"We're just telling you how we feel," said Sonya.

"You're just causing more problems," said Terri.

"Yeah. Here I am, making a major sacrifice for our friendship, and you guys don't appreciate it," Angela reminded them.

Everyone started talking at once. Angela yelled to be heard.

"Hey, I've got another idea!"

They stopped talking and stared at her.

"I think we should ask Bobby who *he* likes," suggested Angela. "That will fix the problem."

"Hey, that sounds great!" cried Terri, launching into a handstand in the middle of the floor.

The other girls agreed. Finally, thought Angela, maybe we can get some work done!

"Wait a minute! Who's going to ask him?" asked Dawn.

They all looked at Angela. She gasped in horror. "Oh, no, not me!"

Chapter Twelve

⚜

At dinner that night Mrs. King talked nonstop about Mr. Bugrin. Angela wished her mother would stop seeing him. What if she married him and then Bobby would become her stepbrother? Yuck!

"Angie, what's wrong?" asked Mrs. King when she finally stopped talking and noticed that Angela was staring glassy-eyed into the distance.

Angela told her mother her plan to ask Bobby which one of the girls he likes.

"I think you should send him a note, Angie, rather than confronting him," Mrs. King suggested. "That way, he won't be embarrassed."

"That sounds good," said Angela. "I'll write the note right now."

She sat down at the kitchen table and composed a multiple-choice note.

Hi, Bobby, this is Angela. As you know, I like you. I just want to know which one of us girls you like. Angela, Terri, Dawn, Sonya, Linda. Please circle one. I won't make a big deal out of it or embarrass you in front of your friends. I just want to know.

She copied it carefully on a piece of yellow stationery and put it in an envelope.

At acting class on Thursday Angela sneaked over to the coat rack. She pushed the letter deep into Bobby's jacket pocket so it didn't fall out.

She had planned to tell her friends about the note, but they didn't have any time together during the past couple of days because they were taking special yearly tests.

Before Angela could tell anyone, Terri had grabbed her and was pushing her in front of Bobby. Angela was so close she was stepping on his feet.

"Tell him," Terri ordered.

"No!" said Angela between gritted teeth. She backed away from him.

"Stampeding me again, huh?" said Bobby, grinning at her.

Angela shook her head and turned away from him.

"We want to talk to you after class," Terri told Bobby.

He blushed. "Okay."

Terri caught up with Angela. "Chicken," she said.

"I wanted to handle it my way, Terri," replied Angela. "I wrote a letter—"

Angela didn't finish because Ms. Bergman called the class to order just then. She went through the motions in class, but as soon as it was over, she rushed to the coat rack to retrieve her letter.

"What're you doing, Angie?" Bobby asked. "Looking for something?"

Angela whirled around. She knew what it looked like—like

she was stealing something from him! "Oh, Bobby, uh—I was—there's something in your pocket that I know about that you shouldn't see."

"What? A bomb?" he asked jokingly.

Just then Terri tugged on his sleeve. "Bobby, come outside, okay?" He grabbed his jacket and she dragged him along behind her. He continued to look over his shoulder at Angela.

Angela trailed them out, feeling a lump start to form in her stomach. Dawn, Sonya, and Linda were waiting for them in the parking lot.

"Okay, Bobby. Which one of us do you like?" asked Terri bluntly.

Bobby's eyes grew wide and he blushed about ten shades of red. The girls giggled nervously, all except Angela, who could barely breathe.

Bobby cleared his throat and said, "I'm sorry, girls. But I'm not ready for a serious relationship yet. I'm only twelve. I guess I have to say I like all of you—as friends," he added quickly.

Angela looked at him in amazement. Where did he learn to talk like that? she wondered. He was so together.

Since Angela had decided she was going to stop liking Bobby, she wasn't totally crushed. It was easier not to think about him at all. The only problem now was that her multiple-choice letter was still in his pocket! If he read it, he would probably never speak to her again. Especially since he already said he didn't want a "serious relationship."

A few nights later Angela was studying in her room when her mother stormed into the house after a date with Mr. Bugrin.

Mrs. King went straight to the kitchen to make some hot chocolate. "Men!" she exclaimed aloud.

"Mom, what's wrong?" Angela asked, joining her.

"Ross Bugrin doesn't want a serious relationship right now, because he just went through a divorce," she said, dumping three giant tablespoons of chocolate into her hot milk.

"Well, maybe he'll change his mind after a while," said Angela comfortingly.

"Maybe, but I may not be around by that time," said Mrs. King.

Secretly, Angela was glad her mom wouldn't be dating Mr. Bugrin anymore, because it was embarrassing. But it annoyed her that Bobby had used his father's exact words when he told her and her friends he liked all of them the other day. She had thought he was so great for saying that about the "serious relationship," but now she thought he probably heard his father practicing it.

Angela didn't see or hear from Bobby for several days. He didn't come to acting class on Monday, and someone said he had the flu. She wondered if he'd read her letter, and maybe he hadn't come to class because he was too embarrassed. She really hoped he'd lost the letter.

The next rehearsal of the Monster Skit went well. Angela decided not to mention the letter to her friends, even though she was still worried about it.

"You were right, Angela," said Linda. "Asking Bobby who he liked solved the problem. Now we don't have any reason to fight over him since he likes all of us the same."

"Just think. You did it all for us," commented Terri, patting Angela on the back."

"A true friend," said Dawn.

"I began to realize that he wasn't all that wonderful," admitted Sonya. "I think his eyes are too close together, for instance."

Angela put her fist up to her mouth as though it were a microphone. "You just heard it, folks, from the girl who wrote the Monster Skit—about how beauty shouldn't influence us."

"I'm glad we're not fighting over you-know-who. It just proves that boys really do get in the way of girls' progress, if you let them," declared Dawn.

"Just what is that supposed to mean?" demanded Howard, who just happened to overhear Dawn's part in the conversation.

"She means those boys who stand outside the girls' rest rooms and won't let the girls get in," said Angela, covering for her friend.

The girls laughed. Howard shook his head in confusion.

"Congratulations, though," he added. "You made it through a whole rehearsal without arguing."

Angela and her friends linked arms and stood in front of him in a row.

"We deserve brownie buttons," said Angela, beaming. If it hadn't been for her plan to ask Bobby whom he liked, she guessed they would still be fighting.

Chapter Thirteen

On the day of the Spring Fling Talent Show, Angela and her friends arrived at school an hour early so they could rehearse one last time.

When they were done, Angela made sure all the things were together that they would need for their skit: the scenery Dawn had painted (complete with animals); the choir robes from Linda's basement and costumes Terri's mother had lent them; the operating room props. But she couldn't find the masks anywhere.

For twenty minutes she searched the backstage area, asking all the kids she ran into if they had seen the masks.

Finally she went to her friends and told them about the missing masks. "I think somebody stole them."

Dawn's eyes grew wide. "Oh, no, what'll we do? The skit won't be the same without masks!"

"I know. Let's split up and search the auditorium. We just have to find them," said Terri with determination.

The five girls headed off in different directions. After having no luck, Angela decided to open all the doors in the hall and search the rooms, too. She opened the door to the first room. Stumbling over something hard, she landed flat, got up, felt for the light switch, and screamed very loudly.

Standing before her was a chamber of horrors. Three naked mannequins were lined up, each wearing a horrible, bloody, distorted mask! Everyone must have heard Angela scream, because people came running from every direction. The room filled with their screams.

Angela noticed that everyone was screaming except Celia and Polly. They only smiled.

"I'll bet you did this," accused Angela.

"Prove it," challenged Celia, gliding away in a pirate costume with gold coins sewn on the front. No pirate would be caught dead in that outfit, thought Angela.

Angela couldn't do anything about Celia then because the show had to go on.

"Oh, no! Come on, only five minutes till showtime!" gasped Sonya, yanking the masks off the mannequins. "Let's go!"

They rushed back to the dressing rooms and helped one another get ready. Finally they were all dressed in their robes and stepped out of the dressing room just in time to see a giant brightly painted cardboard boat being pushed slowly onto the stage. Celia's secret scenery had just arrived.

She heard the auditorium filling up with parents, faculty, and students, and got ready to welcome everyone and announce the first act.

Because Celia's boat was so big and hard to move, her *Pirate of Penzance* skit was put first.

Angela stood in the center of the stage and took a deep breath. "Hi, I'm Angela King. I'm glad you all could make it tonight. Welcome to our Spring Fling Talent Show. Our first act will be . . ."

The curtain opened on Celia, Polly, and Jeannie sitting in the boat in their pirate outfits. They started by singing a jolly song, bobbing their heads back and forth in time to the music. But after one chorus the boat started to crumple when Jeannie and Polly leaned together against the far side. Slowly all three girls disappeared from sight, as if they were being pulled underwater. Soon only their legs were sticking out. Celia, Jeannie, and Polly yelped and screamed, and the audience roared with laughter.

Celia, never one to keep quiet, clambered out of the wreckage and started yelling at Polly and Jeannie.

"If only you hadn't leaned on that side at the same time," she cried.

"But Celia, look! Everybody loves us," Polly pointed out, turning her around to face the audience.

She was right. They were a big hit. Celia instantly changed and put on her biggest, most phony smile. The three girls began their song again and the audience went wild.

When their act was over, it took several minutes for them to push the boat offstage. Finally, it was time for the Monster Skit.

The curtain opened on Sonya running around the stage, flapping her arms as if they were wings to scare the Ugly-faces, Dawn and Linda. Just then, Sonya tripped over a microphone wire and fell flat on her face. She picked herself up and grinned at the audience, who applauded. Angela and Terri stood in a corner talking about what they were going to do to the ugly ones.

Eddie had made the backdrop look like a hospital examining room. Dawn lay on the card table, which was supposed to be a surgery table. Just as Terri was about to operate on her, Terri's mask fell off. The crowd laughed.

"Oh, wow, now you're one of us!" cried Dawn, giggling.

"That is not part of the script, pinhead," hissed Terri, turning bright red. She grabbed her mask and stuck it back on her face, dropping her rubber knife on the floor. She picked up the knife and held it over her head.

"Away with ugliness!" she shouted. "From now on, everybody around here is going to be beautiful like me."

The stage darkened, Dawn shrieked, and a few minutes later, the lights came back on again. Dawn was wearing a mask like Terri's.

"You look much better, Globface," Terri told Dawn.

Then Linda danced out of the shadows, chanting, "You can't catch me, you can't catch me."

"Oh, no, another Uglyface. We must change her," said Angela, running after her with a rubber knife.

Linda turned to face her—except she had no face. She had pulled her long blond hair down to form a curtain over her face. "Someone has to be different around here. Somebody has to be ugly. I want to be the ugly one."

"No, we don't want anybody different from us," insisted Sonya, pushing Linda onto the card table.

The stage darkened. "Just think, we won't call you Hairface anymore. You are one of us," said Angela. It took every ounce of her strength not to burst out laughing.

Linda leaped up from the table. "Oh, no, I'm not one of you! And I never will be!" She grabbed the knife out of Angela's hand. "This is the one time ugliness is going to triumph over beauty!"

"Long live the Uglyfaces!" cried Dawn.

Linda danced just out of reach of the three masked girls. "Accept us the way we are because we're here to stay!" She grabbed Dawn's hand and the two girls chased the others offstage. In the darkness, Terri's voice boomed out, "Hey— maybe the Uglyfaces aren't so bad after all."

The audience laughed and applauded wildly. The lights came on and Angela, Terri, Dawn, Linda, and Sonya stood together and bowed. They were a success!

A few minutes later Howard got up and did his monologue, "A Day in the Life of a Hamster." He was dressed in a brown leotard, with a stubby tail and long whiskers. Everyone went into hysterics at the sight of him.

"I wake up at night and eat a few sunflower seeds, or fresh lettuce—if there is any," he said, twitching his nose. He had taped pipe cleaners to his face for whiskers. "Then I get on my wheel and do a few laps. And maybe I run through my Habitrail. Life is a lot of fun when you're a hamster. You don't have a lot of responsibilities. Sometimes in the morning, my owner picks me up and strokes my soft fur and I waddle all over him, sniffing . . ."

The crowd went crazy. Howard did a great hamster imitation.

After the show Angela and her friends changed into their regular clothes. Angela walked out to the front of the stage and saw Bobby standing there.

"What're you doing here?" she asked him.

"I came to see your skit, and I wanted to see the school, because I'm thinking of transferring here," he answered, grinning at her. "You were great, Angie."

She blushed. It was nice to hear praise from him. "Thanks."

Angela didn't hear Terri, Linda, Dawn, and Sonya sneaking around behind the curtains.

He handed her the letter she had put in his pocket a few days earlier. "Read this."

She looked at him for a minute, and then unfolded the letter. There was her own name circled. She stared at it for a long time just to be sure.

"Why did you tell us you didn't want a serious relationship?" she asked him.

"Because I didn't want to say I liked you in front of all your friends," he told her. "But I liked you from the start. I think it was your hard head that convinced me."

"Really?" she said happily. "Wow, I wonder what my friends will say now."

"We'll say congratulations, right, gang?" asked Terri, popping out from behind the curtains. Angela jumped at the sight of her friend.

"Yeah!" Sonya, Dawn, and Linda chorused, quickly crowding around Bobby and Angela. Obviously, the friends had heard every word of their conversation.

Bobby and Angela turned bright red. Gently, he rapped her on the head with his knuckles.

Celia noticed Bobby just then and wandered over to see what was going on.

"Just who are you?" she asked Bobby, batting her eyelashes.

"Nobody you know," Terri told her.

Then Linda, Terri, Dawn, and Sonya pushed Celia back against the stage curtain. Angela watched, laughing, as her friends wound the thick curtains around Celia.

Celia shouted in protest, but her cries were muffled by the thick material as the girls wrapped her up like a mummy. They didn't let her go until Angela and Bobby were safely out of the auditorium.

About the Author

SUSAN SMITH was born in Great Britain and has lived most of her life in California. She began writing when she was thirteen years old and has authored a number of successful teenage novels, including the *Samantha Slade* series published by Archway paperbacks. Currently, she lives in Brooklyn with her two children. Both children have provided her with many ideas and observations that she has included in her books. In addition to writing, Ms. Smith enjoys travel, horseback riding, skiing, and swimming.

Look for Best Friends #7:

One Hundred Thousand Dollar Dawn,

coming in March 1990

Dawn never imagined winning $100,000 on the game show "Family Fortune" could cause so much trouble! Her family is on a spending spree, people are constantly asking for loans, and Lyle Kraus follows Dawn everywhere. It's up to Dawn and her friends to save the Selby family's Fresh Bakery and solve the problem of being rich.